Praise for Kate Hoffmann
from *RT Book Reviews*

The Charmer

"Hoffmann's deeply felt, emotional story is riveting.
It's impossible to put down."

Your Bed or Mine?

"Fully developed characters and perfect pacing
make this story feel completely right."

Doing Ireland!

"Sexy and wildly romantic."

The Mighty Quinns: Ian

"A very hot story mixes with great characters
to make every page a delight."

Who Needs Mistletoe?

"Romantic, sexy and heartwarming."

The Mighty Quinns: Teague

"Sexy, heartwarming and romantic...a story to
settle down with and enjoy—and then re-read."

Blaze

Dear Reader,

Can you believe it? I've found another Quinn family and this time, they're living in Seattle. Isn't it amazing how these handsome Irish-American guys turn up, just when I need them?

I've lost count of how many Quinn books I've done, but it's been quite a saga, moving from the U.S. to Ireland and Australia and then back to the U.S. again. This new addition to the family story introduces Dermot Quinn, a high-powered Seattle yacht salesman. Only, in this book, you won't catch him in any West Coast boardrooms. No, Dermot's on a journey, one instigated by his wily grandfather. And his destination is a place very dear to my heart, my home state of Wisconsin. I've always wondered if I could set a Harlequin Blaze book on a farm and now you'll see that I have. Yes, a farm can be a very sexy place.

But Dermot isn't the only Quinn on this quest. His brothers, Cameron, Kieran and Ronan, will suddenly find themselves out of their comfort zones, as well—and they'll love every minute of it. Watch for their books in September, October and November of this year.

Until next time, happy reading!

Kate Hoffmann

Kate Hoffmann

THE MIGHTY QUINNS: DERMOT

HARLEQUIN®
entertain, enrich, inspire™

Recycling programs
for this product may
not exist in your area.

ISBN-13: 978-0-373-79706-6

THE MIGHTY QUINNS: DERMOT

Copyright © 2012 by Peggy A. Hoffmann

ABOUT THE AUTHOR

Kate Hoffmann began writing for Harlequin Books in 1993. Since then she's published sixty-five books, primarily in the Harlequin Temptation and Harlequin Blaze lines. When she isn't writing, she enjoys music, theater and musical theater. She is active working with high school students in the performing arts. She lives in southeastern Wisconsin with her cat, Chloe.

Books by Kate Hoffmann

HARLEQUIN BLAZE

HARLEQUIN SINGLE TITLES

Prologue

DERMOT QUINN buried his face in his pillow, fighting back tears. He wasn't going to cry. Nine-year-old boys didn't cry. And if he cried, then that was just admitting that he believed his parents were dead. He squeezed his eyes tightly shut. "Don't cry," he murmured. "Don't cry."

He heard a sound at the door and sat up, brushing an errant tear from his cheek. His twin brother, Kieran, slipped inside the room and shut the door behind him. He crossed to the bed and sat down on the edge.

"He's wrong, you know," Dermot said stubbornly.

"How do you know?"

Dermot shrugged. "Because. They can't be dead. I think they're coming back. We'll be getting ready for school and they'll walk in the door. I know it."

His parents, Jamie and Suzanne, had left four months ago from Seattle, the two of them sailing a yacht that the family boat business had built for a wealthy customer in Australia. They were due to meet up with the owner in Vanuatu six weeks later.

It was supposed to be a family trip, but they'd left early when the owner decided to change the delivery date. Dermot and Kieran, along with their eleven-year-old brother, Cameron, and seven-year-old brother, Ronan, would live with their grandfather for the last month of school.

Dermot wiped his runny nose with the back of his hand. He crossed his legs in front of him. "What do you think happened?"

Kieran considered his answer. "I think they're on an island somewhere. Waiting for someone to find them. There was a storm…or—or a whale…and they got in their life raft before the boat sank."

Kieran had always told the truth and if he believed, then Dermot had hope.

"The life raft washed up on shore in the middle of the night," Dermot said. "And when the sun came up, Da got out and looked around. The island was big, with a thick jungle in the center and white sand beaches. They still had the fishing kit from the life raft. Da fishes while Mom hunts for fruit. Bananas and coconuts. They build a little hut from sticks and palm leaves. And they build a signal fire on the beach so that they'll be ready when another boat sails past."

Kieran nodded. "Yeah. That's it. They're just waiting." He drew a ragged breath. "Do you think they miss us?"

"Yeah," Dermot said. "Sure they do. But they'll be back."

"Promise?"

"Promise," Dermot said.

The bedroom door opened again and they both turned to see their older brother, Cameron, standing in the wash of light from the hall, Ronan peering out from behind him. "Grandda wants us to go over to our house and pick up some of our things."

Dermot scrambled off the bed. "We're not going to live in our house anymore?"

Cameron shook his head. "We're going to live here with him. He said he'll find someone to move our bedrooms over. And our other stuff, too."

"What about Ma and Da's stuff?" Ronan asked.

"I don't know," Cameron said. "I was afraid to ask him. I don't think he wants to talk about it. You know how he is. 'Chin up, lad. Don't want ta have ta care for a babby.'" Cameron did a perfect imitation of their grandfather's thick Irish accent. "We'll be all right," he said.

Dermot slowly crossed the room and stood next to Cameron. Kieran joined them a few seconds later. "We're on our own now, lads," Cameron said, wrapping his arm around Ronan's shoulders. "We need to be strong and brave and we need to pray every single night that this is just a bad dream and that we'll all wake up very soon."

1

DERMOT QUINN was in the middle of a very vivid dream when incessant knocking interrupted him. He slowly opened his eyes, groaning at the morning light that streamed through the bedroom windows of his houseboat. It was a sunny day in Seattle and though he was usually loath to waste good weather, Dermot turned onto his stomach and pulled the pillow over his head.

The subtle scent of a woman's perfume teased at his nose and he pushed up, frowning. Kelly had spent the night last night. They'd met up, as they did on occasion, had a few drinks and come back to his place for a night of NSA sex. Dermot glanced over at the bedside clock. As was her custom, she usually left at dawn for her regular early-morning workout, neatly avoiding any uncomfortable conversation about the night before.

But then, maybe she'd decided to come back for

another few hours of fun. Dermot grinned and threw off the covers. He pulled on a pair of jeans that were tossed over the end of the bed, then walked to the front door. Though he and Kelly followed a very well-honed set of rules, he wasn't averse to breaking them occasionally.

"You could have left the door unlocked," he called as he pulled it open.

But Kelly wasn't waiting on the other side. Instead, he was treated to the sight of his twin brother, Kieran, glaring at him impatiently. "Jaysus, man, do you never answer your cell phone? I've been calling you for the past hour."

"I turned it off," Dermot said. "What are you doing here? It's Saturday morning. Don't you ever sleep in?"

"Get dressed," Kieran ordered. "I got a call from Grandda. He wants to see us all in fifteen minutes. In his office."

"On a Saturday?"

Kieran nodded. "Yeah, I know. Something's up and I'm worried."

"What do you think it is?"

"Hell, I don't know. Grandda's been shut up in his office all week. I'm thinking that he might have gotten an offer on the business."

Dermot and his three brothers had worked for Quinn Yachtworks since they were kids. They all started out sweeping the floors and running materials between the warehouse and the shop. Their grandfather, an Irish immigrant, had founded the firm in the early seventies. A widower with a two-year-old son to care for, he'd arrived in the U.S. a week after Kennedy had been inaugurated, ready to make a life for himself and his motherless son.

After the disappearance of their parents, it was assumed that the business would be left to Cam, Kieran, Dermot and Ronan once their grandfather retired. But Martin had been reluctant to name one of the boys CEO, causing the brothers to wonder what the plan might be.

"You don't think he's sick, do you?" Dermot asked.

Kieran frowned. "What makes you say that?"

"I don't know. He's seventy-seven years old. People get sick when they're older."

"Don't say that." Kieran shook his head. "Don't even think that. He's fine. We'd know if there was something wrong. We'd see it." He strode through the house to Dermot's bedroom, then picked up a shirt from the floor and tossed it at his brother. "Get dressed. We're going to pick up Cameron on the way and talk about this before we go to the meeting."

"What about Ronan?"

"He's already over there."

"What do we have to talk about? We don't know what he's going to say."

"We can guess," Kieran said. "If he plans to sell, we have to work up a counteroffer."

"Do we really want to do that?"

"Yes!" Kieran said. "You want to keep your job, don't you?"

In truth, Dermot hadn't really thought much about it. He liked working for the company. It paid well, it gave him the freedom to come and go as he pleased. As the director of sales, he had a chance to travel and meet interesting—and very wealthy—people. It wasn't what he'd dreamed of as a kid, but childhood dreams didn't pay the mortgage. What wasn't there to like?

Kieran ran the financial end of the business. He'd always been the organized one, the one who could maintain a laserlike focus on the bottom line. Cameron, their older brother, headed the design department, handling the details of what a Quinn-built yacht looked like. And Ronan supervised the manufacturing end of things.

Between the four of them, they were able to do almost any job in the company, and under their management, the business had thrived. "Maybe he's trying to decide who will be in charge," Dermot suggested as he pulled on his T-shirt. "We can't all have the final say on all decisions."

"Maybe," Kieran said. "So, who do you think should be the one?"

"Me," Dermot said, knowing full well the answer would irritate his brother. Of course, Kieran was the one who had the best sense of how the company operated as a whole. But then, without Cameron, the true creative genius behind the designs, the company probably wouldn't be such a success.

"Without sales, the company wouldn't survive," Dermot said. "If you can't sell boats, what do you have?"

"You don't have a clue how the Yachtworks runs," Kieran said. "You'd have us bankrupt in a year."

"Cameron thinks he should be in charge," Dermot said. "Maybe he should. Without his design talent, we'd be in trouble. I'm not sure Ronan even cares, one way or another."

"Are you saying I'm replaceable?" Kieran asked.

"Not as replaceable as I am."

"It's Cameron, then. We both agree. If it comes down to that today, it's Cameron."

Dermot slipped into his boat shoes then nodded. "Let's go find out."

The drive from Dermot's Lake Union houseboat to his brother's home in the Queen Anne neighborhood took ten minutes. Cameron was waiting for them, seated on the front steps of the bungalow. He hopped in the back of Kieran's BMW and had barely closed the door before jumping into the conversation. "What do you think this is about?"

"It could be nothing," Dermot said. "Why are we even speculating? Maybe he just wants us to sign some papers. Or maybe he's finally decided to take a vacation."

"That might be it," Kieran said. He paused, then

shook his head. "He's spent his life building the company. He loves work. Why would he start traveling now?"

"He's always talked about sailing around the world," Cameron suggested.

They passed the rest of the ride in silence, each one of the brothers caught up in his own thoughts as they headed toward the Yachtworks. Dermot wasn't sure which theory he subscribed to.

His grandfather had rarely summoned them all to his office at the same time. The last time it had happened he'd announced that the company would be building a new addition to the finishing department. But with the economy in a downturn, Dermot doubted there would be news of that sort to convey.

The chain-link gates were open when they arrived, and Kieran steered the car through them and parked in front of the main offices next to Ronan's SUV. Quinn Yachtworks was located along the Salmon Bay waterway, a perfect location for launching the luxurious sailboats that they built. They'd become one of the most successful custom builders on the West Coast, with business moguls, sports stars and Hollywood celebrities as clients.

Their grandfather's faithful executive assistant, Miriam, was sitting at her desk when they arrived. As always, she greeted them stoically, giving no clue what awaited them inside the wood-paneled doors.

"Sit," Martin said as they walked in, shuffling the

papers on his desk as he spoke. Ronan looked up from his spot on the leather sofa, his gaze filled with concern. "I expect you're wondering why I've called this meeting, so I'll get right to it." He leaned back in his well-worn leather chair. "Our corporate attorney has advised me that it is time for me to start thinking about my successor."

Dermot watched a strange expression settle on his grandfather's wrinkled face. Martin Quinn was not the kind of man who liked to be reminded of his mortality and this was no exception. Dermot cursed silently. "You're not going to retire, are you?"

"Not tomorrow. But he's right," Martin continued. "It's time to put my affairs in order."

"Is everything all right?" Cameron asked. "I mean, are you well?"

"Fit as a fiddle," Martin said. "But there are practical reasons for this decision. When your parents died, I brought you boys to work with me. You spent your afternoons and weekends learning the business, instead of doing things you wanted to do. You see, I thought it was the best way to deal with your grief. Now I see it was the best way to deal with *my* grief."

"We liked working here, Grandda," Kieran said.

"But you all had your own dreams. Dermot, I remember you wanted to be a veterinarian. And, Cam, you wanted to be an archaeologist."

"Paleontologist," Cameron corrected.

Martin nodded. "Right. And Kieran, you wanted to be a… Well, I don't recall, but—"

"A cowboy," Kieran said. "Or a Royal Canadian Mounted Policeman."

Their grandfather nodded. "And, Ronan, I think all you ever wanted was to have your parents back again. The point is, I never gave you the chance to follow those dreams. And now that I have to decide whether to leave this business to you or sell and make all of us extremely wealthy, I realize that you might not be prepared to make a decision about your future. I don't want any of you to tie yourself to a business that isn't part of your own dreams."

Kieran shook his head. "Grandda, we would never—"

"Let me finish." He folded his hands on his desk and looked at them individually. "I came to this country with one hundred dollars in my pocket and the intention of making something of my life so that I could support my son. I made my own life, something you boys haven't had the chance to do."

"We love working for you," Cameron said. "It's a family business and family sticks together."

"That's a lovely sentiment," Martin replied. "But it doesn't make my decision any easier. So, I have a plan. I'm going to give each of you boys one hundred dollars cash, a company credit card and a bus ticket. I want you to go out there and spend some time in the real world. Find a job. Meet new people. See what life is like all alone in the world. Believe me, without all the comforts of home, you'll have time to figure out what you really want out of life."

Dermot opened his mouth to protest, but his grandfather held up his hand. "Give yourself six weeks. If you're still interested in running the Yachtworks after that, I'll be satisfied."

Cameron gasped. "You're kidding, right? You just expect us to take six weeks away from work? I have projects going."

"Although we'd all like to think we're indispensable," Martin said, "if one of us fell off the planet tomorrow, the company would go on." He stood and handed each of them an envelope.

"You have tonight to pay your bills and put your affairs in order," Martin said. "You leave tomorrow morning. Go out and imagine a different life for yourselves, boys. And when you come back, come back with a decision."

"Vulture Creek, New Mexico?" Cameron asked.

Dermot opened his envelope and withdrew his bus ticket. "Mapleton, Wisconsin. What the hell is in Mapleton, Wisconsin?"

"Bitney, Kentucky," Kieran muttered. "Great."

"Sibleyville, Maine. Jaysus," Ronan said. "I'll be on the bus for a week."

The brothers looked at each other, shaking their heads.

Martin smiled. "Good luck. And I'll see you in six weeks."

RACHEL HOWE grabbed the fifty-pound bag of feed, wrapping her arms around it and lugging it to the back of the pickup truck.

"You need some help with that, little lady?"

She glanced over at the two old men watching her from their spot on the front porch of the local feed store. "Nope," she said, forcing a smile as the bag began to slip through her arms. "I've got it."

Wincing, she took a deep breath and heaved the sack toward the tailgate of the truck. But at the last second, it fell out of her arms and dropped onto her foot. Rachel cursed, then kicked the sack. How would she ever make this work? She couldn't even load a pallet of feed bags onto the truck, much less run a farm with absolutely no help beyond her eighty-year-old uncle.

She was virtually alone in this, with nothing but her determination to keep her company. Her father had maintained the dairy until the day he'd died and he hadn't had help. If a seventy-five-year-old man had managed, certainly his twenty-five-year-old daughter could.

Though she'd put a help-wanted notice in the grocery store and in the feed store, hoping to find a high school boy to relieve her of the heavy lifting, there hadn't been any takers. Her father's bachelor brother, Eddie, was still able to help with the milking but the heavy work was beyond his capabilities.

Maybe all the potential workers knew what everyone else in Mapleton knew—that without help, Rachel's time as a dairy-goat farmer was going to be short-lived at best. Maybe they were right. Maybe she ought to just sell and get on with her own life. A surge of temper caused her face to flush and she reached for the sack again, determined not to fail in front of two more doubters—Harley Verhulst and Sam Robson.

"Are you sure we can't give you a hand?" Harley asked.

"No," Rachel snapped. "It's just going to take me a while to work up my strength."

"A little girl like you shouldn't be running that farm all by your lonesome," Sam commented. "You need to find yourself a husband."

"Preferably one with very big muscles," Harley added.

A husband? Right now she'd be satisfied with one reasonably handsome, completely naked man to tend to her sexual needs once a week. She was quite willing to work out some kind of barter, maybe do his laundry or iron his shirts. It could be a mutually beneficial arrangement.

Rachel gritted her teeth and grabbed the feed sack again, this time using her sexual frustration for extra strength. When she got it up on the tailgate of the pickup, she smiled to herself. But when she looked over at the pallet, she cursed.

From now on, she'd get the feed mill to deliver her supplies, eliminating the need to pretend she knew what she was doing. Though it might be tough to work into the budget, she'd find a way. Rachel wasn't ready to concede defeat. Not yet.

She glanced over at the two men and sent them a withering look. "Do you two plan to stand there pestering me or do you have work to do? Your wives will be happy to know you've taken such an interest in my dilemma. I'll be sure to tell them how helpful you were the next time I see them at the grocery store."

Chastened, the two farmers wandered back inside the co-op, leaving Rachel to tend to her business in solitude. She turned her attention back to the pallet of feed sacks, knowing that it might not be possible for her to load them all onto the truck by herself—at least by sundown. But she was going to die trying. "Just think about sex," she muttered to herself. "And how little of it you've had in the past year."

"Can I give you a hand?"

Rachel spun around, ready to decline the offer with a curt dismissal. But the man standing behind her smiled and her breath caught in her throat. She felt a bit light-headed, then realized it was time to draw another breath.

He was dressed in a comfortable shirt and jeans, clothes that hugged a slender, but muscular body. In his right hand, he carried an expensive leather duffel. She glanced at his shoes and noted that they were expensive, too. Not the kind of wardrobe usually found outside the feed store.

"Are you all right?" he asked.

Gosh, he was handsome, she mused as she looked back into his pale blue eyes. Dark hair that was just long enough to make him look a bit dangerous. A perfectly straight nose and a smile that sent a flood of warmth racing through her bloodstream.

Sex, she thought to herself. As if she'd wished it and it had just appeared. Rachel had long ago come to the conclusion that there weren't any interesting men in all of Walworth County. But obviously one had managed to sneak over the border from Illinois and was now standing directly in front of her.

"Oh, my." Rachel swallowed hard, then reached down to pick up the next bag of feed. She'd be just fine once he stopped staring at her. "You're obviously lost," she said, shaking her head. "Or you're just a figment of my imagination."

"What?"

Rachel glanced over her shoulder. "Men that look like you don't live in places like this." She straightened. "If you just take this road right here out to Highway 39 then stay on 39, it will take you to the interstate. You'll be back in Chicago in a few hours."

"Why do you think I'm from Chicago?"

"You have *big city* written all over you," she said. "Mostly it's the shoes. And the duffel." She bent again to grab a feed sack, but he stopped her.

"Allow me," he said, dropping his duffel in the

dusty parking lot. He picked up the sack, then easily tossed it onto the bed of the truck. "Another?"

"Yes," she said, the word coming out on a rush of air. "Thank you." She pointed in the direction of the pallet. "All of them have to go. Here, let me give you a hand."

"No problem," he said. "You must have some hungry cows."

"Goats. I raise goats."

"Interesting," he said. "I've never met a goat farmer before. Then again, I don't know any cow farmers either."

A laugh burst from Rachel's lips. "Sorry. I know you're trying to be polite. It's just that some days goat farming is far from interesting." She stepped back as she watched him hoist another sack into the truck. "I run a small dairy. It belonged to my family—my grandparents first, and then my father. And—and now it belongs to me."

"Are you Rachel, then?" he asked.

She blinked in surprise. Did she know him? Was he some forgotten classmate from high school? An older brother of one of her friends? A friend of one of her older siblings? "I am."

"I saw your note posted over at the grocery store. One of the checkers told me she saw you pass by and thought you might be headed here. You're looking for a ranch hand?"

"Farm," she said. "It's a farm, not a ranch."

"I thought you said it was a dairy."

"A dairy...farm." She cleared her throat nervously. Was this man really answering her ad?

"So, do you need a hand? Because I need a job and somewhere to stay."

"You want to work for me?" At first, Rachel couldn't believe her good fortune. But then, as she began to consider his offer, she was forced to contemplate why a man as handsome as this one was willing to take a low-paying job without any chance for advancement and virtually no benefits besides all the free goat's milk he could drink. "You don't look like a guy who's spent much time on a farm."

"And you look nothing like a goat farmer," he said, a teasing smile curling the corners of his mouth. "I'm going to be in Mapleton for six weeks. I need a job to occupy my time. And I need a place to stay, somewhere cheap. I'm willing to work hard if you'll give me room and board and a decent wage."

"How decent?" she asked.

"I don't know. What were you looking to pay?"

"Full-time, I should offer you two hundred a week, plus meals and lodging," she said. "I can afford a hundred a week. Cash. Plus room and board."

"A hundred sounds good to me. As long as the meals are decent." He moved to grab another sack and loaded it into the back of the truck. "All of these?"

She nodded as she studied him shrewdly. No, this couldn't possibly be happening to her. Men like this didn't just drop into her life. There must be something more to his story, maybe something…criminal? "What's your name?"

"Dermot," he said. "Dermot Quinn."

"Where are you from?"

"Seattle." He straightened, rubbing his hands on the front of his jeans. "Is this an interview now? As you can see, I'm strong. I'm pretty smart and handy around the house. I'll do what I'm told, unless I don't agree with it, and then I'll tell you."

"You're good at home repairs?"

He nodded. "I can build you just about anything you'd like if you've got tools and materials. Hell, I could build you a boat."

"I don't need a boat," she said. Rachel looked at him intently. "Is there anything that I should know about you before I offer you this job?"

His eyebrow slowly rose as he gave her a quizzical look. "I…prefer beer to wine. I don't like cooked vegetables. I'm not very good at doing my laundry. And I sleep in the buff. Is that what you're getting at?"

An image of him, naked, his limbs twisted in her bedsheets, flashed in Rachel's mind. "Actually, I was going to ask if you have a criminal record," she said. "But I guess the rest is good to know." She couldn't help but smile at the confusion on his face.

"No!" he said. "Of course not. I've never even had a speeding ticket."

"If you don't have a criminal record, why aren't you looking for a real job? A guy with your...talents?"

"Is this an imaginary job you're offering?"

"No. But I mean a job that pays more than slave wages and doesn't involve cleaning gutters and shoveling goat poop. A job where your pretty face might get you more than three dollars an hour."

"It's a long story," he said. "If you hire me, I promise, I'll explain it all to you."

Though Rachel wasn't sure she ought to believe him, there was something about this man that intrigued her. Yet, for all she knew, he could be a consummate liar...or a con man...or maybe a serial killer. "Hang on," she said.

Rachel ran up the steps of the feed store and poked her head inside. "Harley, Sam, come out here. I need you."

"Finally giving up on those feed bags?" Harley asked.

"No. I need you to be a witness." The two men followed her back outside. Rachel pointed to the man standing behind her truck. "Tell them your name," she called.

"Dermot Quinn."

Frowning, she turned back to Harley and Sam. "See this guy? He's coming to work on my farm. If I turn up the victim of some horrible crime, this is the guy to look for." She glanced back at Dermot. "Where are you from again?"

"Seattle," he said.

"Do you have any identification with you?" Harley asked.

Dermot pulled his wallet from his back pocket and took out his driver's license, then handed it to Rachel. "It's all there. I can give you references if you like. People who'll vouch for my character." He withdrew a business card and held it out to her. "Here. You can call my office."

Harley looked over Rachel's shoulder at the identification. "Looks legit to me. But I'd make him sleep in the barn."

"He looks trustworthy to me," Sam said. "And he's a nice lookin' guy, if you don't mind me sayin'." He wagged his finger at Dermot. "Behave yourself, mister, and we won't have a problem. Get out of hand and old Eddie is likely to shoot you in the ass."

Dermot smiled. "I'll be the model of propriety."

"I don't know what that means," Harley muttered, "but anyone who can use big words like that is probably no one to worry about."

The two farmers wandered back inside. "Who is Eddie?" Dermot asked.

"My uncle. He lives on the farm, too. He's not as bad as everyone says he is. He's just a bit...grumpy. It would be best to avoid him." Rachel rubbed her palms together. "I guess you have a job," she said.

"Then, I guess I'd better finish loading this feed," Dermot replied.

THE RIDE TO THE FARM offered Dermot a chance to find out a little more about his beautiful new boss. Her widowed father had died the previous year and she'd come home three months before his death to help care for him. She had two older brothers and an older sister and had worked as an artist in Chicago.

When she pulled off the road and into a driveway, Dermot's attention turned to his new home. Clover Meadow Farm was right out of the movies with its red barn, fieldstone silo and white clapboard house. The old Victorian sat back from the road, surrounded by a grove of tall maple trees. A smaller stone house stood behind it, a ramshackle porch running the length of the facade.

An old man sat on the porch of the stone house, his wrinkled brow furrowed, his dark eyes observant. A small black goat sat on his lap, also watching warily.

"This is it," Rachel said as she hopped out of the truck.

Dermot grabbed his bag from the back of the pickup before following her across the yard. He felt something tug on his leg and glanced down to find the little goat nibbling at the bottom of his jeans.

He stepped away, but the goat was undeterred. "Hey, cut that out."

"Benny, shoo," Rachel said. She looked at the old man on the porch. "Do not let that goat in the house again, you hear me?"

The old man slowly stood. "I hear you. Who is this?"

"Uncle Eddie, this is Dermot Quinn. I just hired him to help out on the farm. He's got six weeks with nothing to do. I figure we can get him to help us finish some of the repair work around here."

The frown on the old man's face grew deeper. "Dermot Quinn? What kind of name is that?"

"It's Irish," Dermot said.

"Lemme see your hands."

Dermot dropped his bag and approached, holding his hands out, then flipping them palms up. "I'm a hard worker. I'm strong and I'm not afraid to get dirty."

"Can you milk a goat?"

Dermot gasped. "No. But I'm sure I could learn if you showed me how."

"Don't worry," Rachel said. "We don't milk by hand. We have machines for that." She smiled at her uncle. "Eddie, I'd like our new worker to take the bedroom upstairs in your house. Do you have any objections?"

Dermot shook his head. "Hey, I don't want to put you out. I can sleep in the barn if—"

"No problem," Eddie said. "I'll be able to keep an eye on him. You step out of line, mister, and I'll run you off with a load of buckshot in your behind. I've done it before, don't think I haven't."

"Come on," Rachel said, walking up the steps. "I'll show you your room."

She held open the screen door and Dermot followed her inside. They climbed a narrow staircase to the second floor and she pointed to a door on the left.

"Has he really shot someone?" Dermot asked.

"Yes. Shot *at* someone. He wasn't aiming to hit him. Just chase him off."

Dermot frowned. Maybe this hadn't been such a good idea. But as he followed Rachel up the stairs, his gaze fixed on her backside, enhanced by a pair of jeans that hugged her curves. No, he'd definitely made the right choice.

"This is the original farmhouse," Rachel explained. "It was built in 1870 by my great-great-grandparents."

She opened the bedroom door to reveal an old iron bed, covered by a colorful quilt. An overstuffed chair sat in the corner, its upholstery worn, and the wall above the bed was covered with old pictures from the turn of the century. Faded flowered wallpaper covered all four walls. An old chest of drawers and a vanity sat near each of two windows.

"My great-grandparents lived here, too, before they built the big house. My grandparents lived here after my parents took over the farm. My grandfather was born in this room." She drew a deep breath. "It's nothing fancy. No air-conditioning, but I'll bring you a fan from the house."

"I don't need anything fancy," he said. "This is

really quite nice." He'd always heard that farmers' daughters were supposed to be beautiful, but he hadn't expected this.

Though she wore faded jeans and a tattered shirt, Rachel Howe was a stunner. Her honey-blond hair was pulled up into a crooked ponytail and tied with a scarf and she wore absolutely no makeup. Yet, he couldn't take his eyes off her. And obviously farming was good exercise because she had a body that any trainer would be proud of.

"There's a bathroom downstairs," she said. "Just off the kitchen. No shower, just a tub. There are showers in the barn. Probably better to use those rather than upset Eddie's routine."

"He doesn't seem to like me much," Dermot said.

Rachel laughed. "He's not so bad, once you get to know him. And a word of warning. Don't let him talk you into helping him get rid of the skunk living under the corncrib. He's got some kind of vendetta going on, and the last time he got sprayed, he stunk for a week."

"I'll keep that in mind," Dermot said.

"I'll just open a window and get some fresh air in here."

Rachel managed to get one sash up, but struggled with the other. Dermot crossed the room and reached around her to offer his help. But the moment their bodies brushed against each other, he realized how close they actually were. The window flew up and Rachel fell back against him.

Holding on to her shoulders, he turned her around. Their gazes locked for what seemed like an eternity. Though he knew it was probably a mistake, Dermot's instincts took over and he bent close and brushed a kiss across her lips. When she gasped, he quickly stepped back, cursing his impetuous move.

"Sorry," he said. "I'm... I shouldn't have done that." He raked his fingers through his hair and shook his head. "Shit. I don't usually—"

"I liked it," Rachel interrupted.

"What?"

"Don't be sorry. I wanted you to kiss me." Her cheeks flushed and she smiled nervously. "A single woman living on a goat farm doesn't often get the opportunity to kiss an attractive single man." She paused. "You are single, aren't you?"

"Absolutely," he said.

She gave him a dubious stare. "Really?"

Dermot held his hand to his heart. "I swear."

"Oh, my God, why?" she asked. "A guy as good-looking as you could have any woman he wanted."

"I guess I just haven't found the right woman yet."

"Well, you've come to the wrong place," she said with a laugh. "Mapleton, Wisconsin, is not exactly crawling with beautiful women."

"I found one already," Dermot replied. "And I've only been here a few hours."

This brought a deeper blush to her cheeks. "You have the job. You don't have to flatter the boss to keep it."

"You're beautiful, I'm charming. I think we'll get along just fine."

Rachel seemed to enjoy the back-and-forth banter between the two of them and Dermot realized that being stuck in Mapleton, Wisconsin, might not be the worst thing in the world. He had a roof over his head and a sexy woman to occupy his thoughts. If the food were decent, he'd be set.

"Well, I'll let you settle in. We've got a few hours before we start milking. We milk the goats twice a day, 5:00 a.m. and 5:00 p.m."

"Right," he said warily. "I suppose they don't milk themselves."

"Don't worry. You'll be fine." She turned for the door, then glanced over her shoulder. "When you're ready, I'll give you a tour of the barns. Just knock on the back door."

Dermot listened to her footsteps on the stairs, then he heard the screen door slam. He chuckled softly as he shrugged out of his shirt. What was a woman like Rachel doing all alone on a goat farm? Maybe this was his problem. All the really interesting women in the world were living in some rural hideaway, waiting for some unsuspecting guy to discover them.

He unzipped his duffel, then grabbed a clean T-shirt. He stared at his reflection in the old mirror above the chest of drawers. Though he'd spent the past two days on a bus, he didn't look any worse for wear. He was in serious need of a shave and a shower and a decent meal and a long nap. But he suspected all that would have to wait until after he milked a few goats.

Dermot smoothed his hand over the stubble on his cheek. He could at least manage a quick shave. He stripped out of his shirt and then, dressed only in his jeans, grabbed his shaving kit and headed downstairs to the bathroom.

He'd just lathered his face when Eddie appeared at the bathroom door. "I—I was just going to shave. If you prefer I do this in the barn, I can—"

Rachel's uncle scowled, then nodded. "My goats prefer a well-groomed dairyman. But lay off the Old Spice. They won't like you if you smell funny."

As he lathered his face, Dermot watched the old man in the mirror. He had to hand it to his grandfather. This was going to be a real challenge, especially considering that he'd have both a beautiful woman and her surly uncle to contend with.

He wondered whether his brothers had arrived at their destinations and what strange fates had befallen them. Would they be as lucky as he was to find such lovely scenery?

Though he was tempted to call one of them, his grandfather had requested that they give up their cell phones for the duration. They were on their own, left to their own devices to live a different life for the next six weeks.

When he left Seattle, six weeks had seemed like an eternity. But now that he'd met Rachel Howe, it seemed like barely enough time at all.

2

RACHEL STOOD AT the kitchen sink, staring out the window at the front porch of the stone house. Her gaze fixed on a bumblebee that lazily buzzed around her grandmother's perennial garden as her mind wandered back to the kiss she'd shared with Dermot Quinn.

A tiny shiver skittered through her and she turned her attention back to the lunch dishes. How was it possible to be so overwhelmingly attracted to a man she didn't even know? She'd been living at the farm full-time for over a year now, with her friends an hour away in Chicago. She hadn't been with a man in all that time.

"I suppose that explains it," she murmured to herself. Though she'd never call herself promiscuous, she did have boyfriends and lovers on a fairly regular basis. But a year was a really long time to go without any sex at all. And since Dermot had arrived, her year of celibacy seemed destined to end—soon.

It wasn't as if she wanted to live the life of a nun. Leaving the farm was almost impossible, even for a weekend. Eddie couldn't run the dairy on his own and she hadn't been able to find reliable helpers. So she'd been stuck, biding her time and wondering if her sex life would ever get back to normal.

Maybe the solitude had just gotten to her and that's why she'd kissed him. Yes, she was pathetically lonely and he was incredibly handsome and charming. Would it be wrong to take advantage of her good fortune? A kiss here and there wouldn't do either one of them any harm. But could she stop at just one kiss?

A screen door squeaked and she glanced up to see Dermot headed across the yard, freshly shaved and dressed in a faded T-shirt and jeans. Every time she looked at him he seemed to get more good-looking. A few seconds later, he knocked on the door. She grabbed a towel and wiped her hands, then let him in.

"Hey," he said, giving her a shy smile.

"You look…refreshed," Rachel commented. "Are you hungry? I could make you a sandwich. It's going to be a while until dinner. We eat after we're done milking and that's usually around eight."

He nodded. "No, I can wait. I know I haven't earned anything yet but—"

She held out the dish towel. "You can dry the dishes," Rachel suggested.

He chuckled softly. "I may not know how to milk a goat, but I can definitely dry dishes." He took the towel from her hand, his fingers touching hers for a moment. The contact sent a thrill racing through her and she groaned inwardly.

So it had been a year. She still remembered exactly what to do with a man once she had him in bed. It wasn't something she could forget. But a man as sexy as Dermot might expect a woman to please him in very different ways, very…unusual ways.

Though Rachel considered herself experienced, most of the guys she'd been with hadn't been very adventurous in the bedroom. She could count her lovers on two hands with a couple fingers left over. And the most exciting experience she'd ever had was making love on the kitchen floor of her apartment.

She stared at the spot on the floor at Dermot's feet, wondering if that might be the next place it happened.

"Rachel?"

Startled out of her thoughts, she looked up to find him staring at her. "I was just going to make a pie for dessert," she mumbled.

Her heart pounded and she drew a deep breath to try to calm herself. How had this happened? She hadn't even thought of the possibilities until he'd kissed her, and now she could think of nothing else. Her brain was filled with sex, sex and more sex.

"You can bake a pie," he said. "I'm not sure I've ever met a woman who could bake a pie."

Rachel slowly gathered the things she'd need and placed them on the table in the center of the kitchen. That's not all she could do, she mused. In fact, she had a lot of undiscovered talents.

"Tell me what you're doing on this farm all alone."

"I was raised here," she said. "My parents used to keep dairy cows, but I was allergic to cow's milk, so they got some goats. As my dad got older, it was easier to raise goats."

"When did your parents pass away?" Dermot asked.

"My dad just this last fall. My mom about five years ago."

"My folks died when I was just a kid," he said. "In a boating accident."

"I'm sorry," she said, glancing up at him.

He shrugged. "I barely remember them. We were raised by my grandfather. Me and my three brothers."

"I have a sister and two brothers, but they're a lot older than me," she explained. "The closest one is fifteen years older. I don't remember living with siblings. It was always just me and my parents."

"So you stayed on the farm with them?"

She shook her head. "Nope. I did the same thing that my brothers and sister did. As soon as I graduated from high school, I headed out into the world. I went to art school in Chicago and then started my own line of greeting cards. I lived in San Francisco and then moved to New York with a boyfriend, who broke up with me a month later. I came back here to care for my dad and decided to stay for a while." She paused. "My dad's will stipulated that if any of his children wanted to run the farm, then they could have it. If not, it gets sold and the proceeds divided up between us."

He nodded. "I wouldn't want this place sold," he said. "It's perfect."

"You haven't met the goats yet," she said with a smile.

"I met Benny. He was kind of cute."

"It's like living with sixty children who never stop eating, will try anything to get loose, require round-the-clock supervision and can't tell you when they're sick. It can be really stressful at times. I'm just glad to finally have some help."

"Well, anything I can do to relieve your stress, just let me know."

Rachel met his gaze, wondering if he was thinking what she was. There were many ways to relax. A nice, long bath. A massage. A lazy afternoon in bed with a naked man. And an orgasm so powerful that it— Rachel swallowed hard and turned back to the pie.

She could barely remember what she was supposed to do, her hands fumbling with the ingredients. They continued to chat, but all she could think about was finding an excuse to stand close enough to him so he might kiss her again.

Once the pie was in the oven, she went to the sink to wash her hands. He handed her the towel. "What next, boss?"

"You can help me bring the goats in from the pasture. I think we should get an early start on the milking since I'm going to have to teach you how to do it."

"All right," he said. "Let's go. I'm ready to get to work." They walked to the door and he opened it for her, then gently rested his hand on her back as she passed through. Was he feeling the same way about her? Was he looking for an excuse to touch her? Or was she the only lovesick, horny fool on this farm?

As they crossed the yard, he kept a respectful distance. But when they got past the barn to the path out to the west pasture, he grabbed her hand and tucked it in his. Rachel smiled to herself. Maybe he was having a hard time keeping his hands off her.

She tried her best to explain the basics of the dairy, the breeds of the goats, the process for pasteurizing the milk, and the small artisanal-cheese maker who bought the milk from her.

"It's a beautiful place," Dermot said.

"It is," she agreed. "But it's so difficult to make a go of it. We're always scrambling to pay the bills. My sister and brothers want to sell, but I'm just not ready for that yet. I made a promise to my dad to keep the farm in the family. I don't want my generation to be the last generation of Howes to live at Clover Meadow."

As they walked, Dermot continued to question her. Rachel was surprised at how much he was able to absorb about the business aspects of farming. He was exactly the kind of person she needed here on the farm—for so many reasons beyond just sexual.

When they reached the gate of the pasture, Rachel stood on the bottom rung and unwrapped a leather lead from the post. "Watch," she said. She put her fingers in her mouth and whistled. The herd all turned in her direction and started moving toward her.

"Wow, that's amazing. They're like dogs."

"They're really, really smart," she said. She handed him the lead, then opened the gate. "Clip this onto the goat with the bell. That's Lady. She's kind of the queen of the dairy. The oldest goat. I took her to the State Fair my senior year of high school. Blue ribbon. We're very old friends."

"Do they bite?" he asked, observing the herd warily.

"Sometimes. But just walk in there like you know what you're doing. Show them who is boss."

"I don't know what I'm doing," he said.

"Charm them like you charmed me," Rachel suggested.

"And how did I charm you?" he asked, leaning closer.

"Talk sweet to them. Soft. Smile a little."

Rachel ushered him inside the gate, then closed it behind him. The goats surrounded him and he held up his arms as they nudged at his legs. When he spotted Lady, Dermot gradually worked his way over to her and clipped the lead on her collar. "All right, now what?"

"Now lead her to the gate and the rest of the goats will follow."

He did as he was told, and before long they were walking down the lane between the paddocks, chatting about his first success as a dairyman.

"Why do they follow?" he asked.

"They know they're going to get fed."

"Haven't they been eating all day?"

"Yeah, but they get the good stuff in the barn."

"Steak and potatoes?"

"Corn and some pellet feed."

"Yum," Dermot said. "Are we having the same for dinner?"

"I think I can scratch up something a little better. But we still have a lot of work to do before we eat."

"I can handle it," he said. "I've got Lady following me. How much harder can it get?"

DERMOT COULDN'T remember the last time he'd been so exhausted. Once the goats got into the milking shed, the work was nonstop for three solid hours. He barely had a chance to take a breath before Rachel or Eddie was showing him something else that had to be done. Benny, the little black goat, was constantly underfoot, nibbling on Dermot's jeans and the hem of his T-shirt.

Rachel explained that it normally took her four hours to do the milking on her own, but once he got up to speed, she expected they'd be able to do the entire herd in about two hours between the three of them.

Completely spent, he sat down in a rocking chair on the back porch of the house while Rachel was inside taking a shower. He'd grabbed a quick shower in the barn after the chores were done, then found a beer in Rachel's refrigerator.

Dermot took a long drink and closed his eyes. He'd known her for less than a day and she was already the most amazing woman he'd ever met. The work it took to keep the farm running seemed overwhelming and yet she never once complained.

"You put in a good day of work."

He opened his eyes to find Eddie watching him from the bottom of the steps, Benny standing at his side. "Thanks," Dermot said, leaning forward in the chair. "And thanks for showing me the ropes. I appreciate it."

The old man nodded curtly. "Tell Rachel I'm heading into town for dinner. They got bingo at the firehouse tonight and I got some money burning a hole in my pocket."

"You're not having dinner with us?"

Eddie shook his head. "I expect you can manage to eat on your own." He nodded, then put his battered John Deere cap on his head and walked toward the truck, Benny at his heels. A moment later, Eddie and the goat drove out of the yard, leaving a cloud of dust in their wake.

"I didn't know that goats played bingo," Dermot murmured.

He stood and stretched, then walked into the kitchen. The least he could do was help Rachel with dinner. He opened the fridge and began to pick through the contents. A salad would be a good start. She'd pulled three steaks from the fridge and they were sitting on the counter near the sink.

"Potatoes," he said. He found some in a mesh bag beneath the sink. By the time Rachel wandered back into the kitchen, the salad was made, the potatoes were washed and the oven was heating, and he'd poured her a glass of wine.

He handed her the wine, taking in the sight of her. Her hair was still wet, long and loose and curling around her face. She wore a cotton dress, cut deep at the neck. Her feet were bare and she smelled of soap.

"Thanks," she said, glancing at the table. "You've been busy."

"I've decided to make myself invaluable. I am a pretty good cook when it comes to meat and potatoes."

"I'm glad to hear that. There are nights that I'm

just too exhausted to cook and this is one of them." Rachel crossed to the fridge then pulled out a package of cheese and found a bag of crackers. "This is some of the cheese made from our goats' milk," she said, arranging the cheese and crackers on a plate.

They headed back out onto the porch and sat down together in the porch swing. "This is my favorite time of the day," she said. "After everything is done and the sun is going down and it's so quiet that you wonder if anyone is still alive in the world."

"I live on the water in Seattle, so it's never completely quiet."

"Do you have a beach house?"

Dermot shook his head. "A houseboat. It's not actually a boat because you can't take it out on the water. Although my family has a boat. Actually we have three. We build boats."

"That's what you do?"

"I don't build them myself. I sell them."

"Motorboats?"

"No. Luxury sailing yachts."

She frowned. "Why are you here?"

"Because my grandfather decided that my brothers and I weren't given a chance to follow our dreams when we were kids. He gave us a hundred dollars, a credit card and a bus ticket and I ended up here. I'm supposed to live a different life for six weeks and then figure out if I like it better than my old life."

"If you have a credit card, why do you need to work?"

"Because he canceled the credit cards once we all got on the bus. I think he wanted us to work rather than lounge around for six weeks. When I landed in Mapleton, I had exactly six cents to my name. I was lucky to meet you."

"I think I'm the lucky one," she said with a smile.

They stared out at the sunset, watching as it turned pink and then orange and then purple. "Do you ever get lonely out here?" Dermot asked.

"All the time," she said. "But I've kind of gotten used to it. I just can't let this place go yet."

"Why?" he said.

"Because it's all I have left of my parents," she said. "It was always the three of us. I'd help my dad with the chores and we'd raise and show our goats at the county fair. And I'd help my mom in the kitchen. She taught me how to bake and sew and keep house. We shopped for antiques and collected quilts. This is who I am, this place. It's my home and it will be my home until I'm ready to let it go. Does that make sense?"

Dermot remembered how difficult it was for him to let go of his parents, to come to grips with the idea that they were really dead. There were still times when he caught himself wondering if they were alive, stranded on some tiny island in the Pacific, waiting for rescue.

She glanced over at him, and for the second time that day, he decided to kiss her. He leaned forward, waiting for a sign that she'd welcome a kiss. Her gaze fixed on his mouth and her lips parted slightly. As they met, her eyes closed and she sighed softly.

He'd kissed a lot of women for a lot of reasons, but there was something about kissing Rachel that was so perfect. Though they spent hours chatting, they seemed to communicate just as well through their desire. He was learning more about her life, but as she kissed him, he was exploring her heart and soul.

She slipped her hand around his nape as he deepened the kiss, his tongue delving into the warmth of her mouth. She tasted like red wine and hidden need and Dermot wondered how far he could go before she stopped him. He didn't want to take advantage and he knew she'd been alone on the farm for a long time.

His hands spanned her waist and he pulled her closer, anxious to feel her body against his. Rachel seemed just as anxious to touch him and she began to unbutton his shirt. When she'd pushed the fabric aside, she pressed a kiss to the center of his chest.

For a long moment, she didn't move, and Dermot was sure she was going to call an end to the seduction. But then she looked up at him with wide eyes. "Take me to bed," she said. "Right now."

Dermot sucked in a sharp breath, not sure that he'd heard her right. "What?"

"Don't make me say it again, because I'm not sure I'll be able to."

"A-all right."

"And don't ask if I'm sure, because I wouldn't have said it if I wasn't."

"Your place or mine?"

"Mine," she said. She stood and held out her hand, and when he took it, Dermot followed her back inside. She led him up the stairs to a spacious bedroom decorated in blue and yellow. The windows were open and lace curtains fluttered with the evening breeze.

She sat down on the edge of the bed and Dermot sat beside her. He grabbed her hand and brought it up to his lips, pressing a kiss to her wrist. He felt nervous, wondering just how he ought to approach her. Reaching out, he cupped her chin in his hand and brought her gaze to his.

A soft sigh escaped her lips and then she smiled. He felt his nerves ease a bit, and when he kissed her, she surrendered without hesitation. As they fell back onto the bed, he realized that none of the women he'd bedded in the past had meant anything. And yet, this sweet, sexy farm girl had captured his desire in less than a day.

"Bewitched," he murmured, his lips brushing hers.

"What?"

Dermot drew back. "I'm Irish. We believe in all sorts of magical creatures. And I do believe you've bewitched me, Rachel Howe."

"There's no magic at work here," she said. Hooking her fingers through his, she drew his hand to her breast, then pressed it against the soft warmth of her flesh. She wasn't wearing a bra and the thin cotton of her summer dress barely hid what was beneath.

With a soft growl, Dermot stretched out beside her. "How long has it been for you?" he asked.

"Too long," she said. "What about you?"

"I think I've been waiting for you my whole life," he said. He'd always known what to say to seduce a woman. But with Rachel, he didn't want to hand her some cheesy line. He wanted to be completely honest. "Actually, I'm a little nervous."

"You are?" She crawled on top of him and kissed him, lingering over his mouth and tracing the crease of his lips with her tongue. "We'll just go very slowly."

She leaned forward and the front of her dress gaped, giving him a perfect view of her breasts. "That sounds like a good idea. I think maybe I should start with your neck." He pressed his lips to the spot below her ear.

He'd never had so much fun kissing a woman as he did kissing Rachel. They laughed and whispered and rolled around on the bed until they found a comfortable spot, their arms wrapped around each other. But suddenly, she sat up and wrinkled her nose.

"Do you smell something burn—" She groaned. "I left the pie in the oven—"

"And I turned the oven on to bake the potatoes," he said.

Rachel jumped out of the bed and ran for the bedroom door, then turned and pointed to him. "Stay here. Do not move. I'll be right back."

Dermot rolled onto his back and threw his arm over his eyes. A pleasant exhaustion settled over him and he let his thoughts drift. He'd spent last night on a bus somewhere in the Dakotas. He'd jumped off the bus and almost immediately loaded a pallet of feed into Rachel's truck. Then he'd dried dishes, milked a herd of goats and prepared a salad, all the while trying to stop thinking about grabbing Rachel and carrying her to the bedroom. No wonder he was tired.

The next thing he knew, she was beside him again. The room was dark. He wrapped his arms around her and pulled her body against his.

"You fell asleep," she whispered.

"I didn't," Dermot said. "Did you save the pie?"

"It's pretty much inedible. But I'll make another tomorrow."

"Sorry. I didn't think to look inside the oven before I turned it on."

"Close your eyes," she murmured. "You need your sleep. We have to get up in six hours."

Dermot turned his face into her soft hair and inhaled the scent of her. Making love to her would wait. It was enough to lie next to her, to run his hands over her body and kiss her silken skin.

When his grandfather had sent him off, he'd expected to find a little bit of himself along the way. He'd never thought that he'd find a woman, as well. Rachel needed him, and for the next six weeks, he'd do what he could to make her life easier. And if the compensation included sharing her bed, he'd consider the job a success.

3

RACHEL OPENED HER EYES and looked around her bedroom. Frowning, she glanced down to see that she was still wearing her clothes. How had she—

Memories of the night before came rushing into her head. Dermot. They'd fallen asleep in her bed. She rolled over to find his half of the mattress empty. A sick feeling came into her stomach as she considered the possibilities.

Had he left sometime before dawn to return to the stone cottage? Had he gathered his belongings and sneaked away in the dark of night, finished with farm work and the woman who pretended to be his boss? Or maybe he was just an early riser, she mused.

Pushing up on her elbow, she picked up the alarm clock and squinted at the time. "Six-fifteen?" With a cry, Rachel bolted upright and swung her feet over the edge of the bed. She'd overslept! How had she overslept? The alarm was set for four-thirty. She always woke up before it rang.

She tugged her dress over her head and pulled on the first work clothes she could find. Slipping her feet into her shoes, she stumbled to the bathroom and grabbed a band to tie up her hair.

The sun was already well above the horizon as she raced across the yard. It was crucial that she keep a regular milking schedule to maximize yield. After eleven months, she'd never missed milking time— except for today.

"This is exactly what you deserve," she muttered to herself. "A man comes into your life and you forget about all your responsibilities."

With a soft curse, she yanked open the door to the milking parlor. To her shock, a row of goats was lined up on the platform in the midst of being milked. She found Dermot nearby, scattering clean straw on the floor. Eddie and Benny stood to the side, watching him. Dermot glanced up and gave her a little wave as she approached.

"What are you doing?" she demanded.

"My job," he said. Dermot lowered his voice. "You looked so relaxed, I didn't want to wake you. I figured I'd give it a go on my own this morning."

"You can't do this by yourself," she said.

"Sure I can. You taught me what to do last night. It didn't seem too complicated. Eddie's been here to help me along. I mixed and fed them their corn and pellets. I figure I'll just be another hour. You can go back to bed if you like."

Rachel frowned. She could do the whole herd in four hours. How was it possible that he could best her speed after only one lesson? "You must be missing something," she said.

He held out his hands. "Check it out. I'm pretty sure I'm doing it right."

Rachel walked through the parlor, checking all the settings on the machines and going over her regular list of tasks. After a thorough inspection, she was forced to admit that Dermot was right. He'd done his job well.

"All right," she said. "I'm impressed."

His expression of concern was broken by a wide grin. "Yeah. I know what I'm doing."

She glanced over at Eddie and he gave her a wink and a reluctant smile, then walked out of the barn, Benny scampering after him. Was her uncle aware of what was going on between them? How long had Dermot stayed in her bed last night?

Rachel kept her questions to herself as they finished with the last of the goats, washed up in the sinks in the pump room and then walked the herd to the pasture. Rachel stood on the gate as she watched the goats graze, smiling to herself. It was nice to know that she had someone to count on, someone who could take the pressure off her, even if it was just for a few hours.

"There's a kind of comfort in the routine," Dermot said as he stood next to her. "I can understand why people would like this life. And they're so smart. That little Benny is a riot. He jumped up on the ledge in the barn and was leaping around like a circus animal."

"Eddie treats him like a dog. But I draw the line at letting him live in the house."

"Why would you ever want to leave this place?" Dermot asked.

Rachel leaned back, gripping the top rail of the fence. "Sometimes I can see myself staying here. It would be the perfect spot to raise a family." She drew a deep breath. "And then there are moments when I'm so tired I feel like crying. When I feel like there has to be more than milking goats for the rest of my life."

"What do you want? What do you dream for yourself?" Dermot asked, his voice quiet. He reached out and brushed a strand of hair from her eyes, but she quickly turned from the gate and began to stride down the lane, frustration causing emotion to swell in her throat.

He'd just proved beyond a shadow of a doubt that she wasn't cut out for this. What took him just a few hours to learn had taken her a lifetime. The longer she stayed, the more she was coming to realize that her heart just wasn't in it anymore. Yes, this was home, yet it seemed like a weight around her neck, dragging her down into a life she wasn't sure she wanted.

"Hey, wait up," he called. When he caught her, he

reached out and grabbed her hand, but this time Rachel wouldn't allow herself to feel anything. She had six weeks with Dermot's help, six more weeks to get her act together or admit that her siblings were right—running the dairy was no life for a single woman.

"We need to bring some straw down from the barn," she said. No doubt that would take him a few minutes at the most to complete, a job that took her a half hour to do.

"What's wrong?"

"Nothing," Rachel said. "Really. I'm just— I haven't had breakfast and I'm hungry."

"Are you angry that I didn't wake you? I just thought you might like to sleep in for once."

When they reached the barn, Rachel pulled open the huge sliding door and they both walked inside. Usually she was forced to bring the pickup truck around and wrestle the bales of straw and hay up onto the truck bed or break them apart and carry them to the goat pen in pieces.

"I need you to bring four or five bales of straw to the building behind the milk parlor. Drop them down through that trapdoor, then carry them around to the parlor. Can you do that?"

"Sure," he said, frowning.

His gaze searched hers and she knew he was wondering about the sudden shift in her mood. "You need some gloves."

He reached behind him and produced a brand-new pair of leather gloves. "Eddie gave me these this morning."

"Fine," she muttered. "Let's go."

As she stepped away, Dermot grabbed her arm and pulled her close. "There's just one thing we need to take care of first," he said. Wrapping his hands around her waist, he picked her up and drew them both down into a pile of straw.

A huge cloud of dust and chaff rose up around them and Rachel began to sneeze. Dermot sat up and waved his hand in front of him, coughing. When the dust had finally settled, he glanced over at her and chuckled. "That always works in the movies."

Rachel couldn't help but laugh. "What were you planning to do once you got me into the hay?"

He cupped her chin in his hand and kissed her. "This," he murmured. His lips moved to her neck. "And this." He bit her shoulder gently. "And a little bit of this."

He pulled her onto his lap and wrapped her legs around his waist. Rachel closed her eyes and enjoyed the feel of his hands and his mouth on her body. When he moved lower, she held her breath and then his lips teased her nipple beneath the fabric of her T-shirt. Her frustration quickly dissolved and Rachel enjoyed the pleasant sensations pulsing through her body.

He caught the hem of her shirt in his fingers and slowly drew it up, pressing a line of kisses across her belly, bending her back until she felt dizzy with desire.

"Did you forget your underwear this morning, boss?"

"I believe I did," Rachel said.

"Good. It tends to get in the way." A moment later, his mouth came down on her nipple and Rachel gasped, the shock sending currents of pleasure through her body. Her thoughts focused on that small spot, as if he'd found the core of her desire.

It had been so long since a man had wanted her. Furrowing her fingers through his hair, she moved against him, desperate to have him continue his exploration. He took a momentary break to pull off his shirt, giving her a wide expanse of skin to touch.

He had an incredible body, slender, yet muscular, burnished golden by the sun. Rachel imagined what his life was like in Seattle. Though he seemed to fit perfectly on the farm, there was no doubt that his life in the city suited him better.

But that didn't mean he wouldn't remember their time on the farm. She'd make sure he never forgot. She pulled her shirt over her head, then ran her fingers through her tangled hair. "Now what?"

A slow grin curled the corners of his mouth. Holding tight to her, he got to his feet and then set her down. He kicked off his shoes and reached for the button on his jeans.

"Wait," she said. Rachel undid the button herself,

then slowly lowered his zipper. She should have been nervous, but she wasn't. This was exactly what she wanted, what she'd hoped for last night. And now it was happening and she wanted to enjoy every last moment.

She skimmed his jeans down over his hips, his erection tenting the fabric of his boxers. He kicked the jeans away and she moved back up, smoothing her palm along the length of his shaft. He was so hard, so ready.

"Condom," he murmured.

She didn't want to stop now, didn't want to wait. Rachel needed to know how deep his need ran. Slipping her hand into the waistband of his boxers, she wrapped her fingers around him and slowly began to stroke. "We won't need one," she said. "Not right now."

He leaned back against the post and watched her, his gaze shifting between her face and her hand. Rachel knew he was close, and every now and then, he'd draw in a sharp breath and close his eyes, as if fighting off the first tremors of his orgasm.

He seemed to grow harder with each stroke, and Rachel leaned closer, her breasts brushing against his chest. He groaned and then his breath froze. A heartbeat later, his body jerked and Rachel's hand grew slick with his orgasm.

He reached down to stop her and she slowed her pace, pressing her lips to his chest. He shuddered when her tongue circled his nipple, his fingers tangling in her hair.

When he was completely spent, she stepped back and looked up at him. If she thought his desire would be sated, she was wrong. His gaze smoldered, searing her with unhidden need. "I guess that wasn't the way things went in the movies either," she said.

She reached down and picked up her T-shirt. "I think you might need another shower."

"Are you going to come with me?"

"We'll get to that," Rachel said with a sly smile. "We can't do everything in one day."

DERMOT HAD NEVER expected his first full day of work to include a full-scale seduction. But the attraction between him and Rachel was impossible to deny. From the moment he set eyes on her, desire seemed to be at the top of his mind.

Was that so difficult to believe? Every time she looked at him, he was acutely aware that he'd never met a woman quite like her. She was stubborn and determined, yet so vulnerable at the same time.

He'd never met anyone who worked so hard against such high odds. It was clear that the dairy was gradually wearing her down. The work seemed to be endless, without a break. And even the extra rest he'd given her that morning came with emotional consequences.

It was pretty clear that she was torn between family loyalty and whatever dreams she had for her own life. And it was strangely ironic that he was dealing with the same decisions. Dermot wanted to help her, but he was at a loss himself. He just figured that when the time came to make a decision, he'd know exactly what he wanted, no tears, no guilt. Just a simple decision.

He adjusted the extension ladder against the house, then crawled up to the top. Rotted leaves clogged the gutters and he grabbed them by handfuls and let them fall to the ground. After he cleaned the gutters, he had to repair the rail on the front porch, replace a broken pane of glass in an upstairs window and fix the barn door. All before afternoon milking.

"Are you almost done up there?"

He looked down to find Rachel standing at the foot of the ladder. "Almost," he called.

"Good, because you make me nervous up that high."

He climbed down and jumped the last three steps, landing beside her. "Do you have another job for me to do?"

"Yes," she said.

"I'm not done with this job yet."

"It's time for lunch," she said. "I thought we might have a picnic. There's a place I want to show you. It's my favorite place on this whole farm."

"I need to wash my hands and I'll be ready to go."

They returned to the kitchen and Rachel grabbed a

picnic basket and a blanket. He wiped his clean hands on a towel, then took the basket from her. "Lead on," he said.

"Thank you for cleaning the gutters," she said as they walked down the steps. "I tried a couple of times to climb that ladder, but I couldn't get past the sixth step. You're very brave."

"Try hanging from the top of the mast in a bosun's chair under full sail in a choppy sea," he said. "This was nothing."

"I have no idea what you just said," Rachel replied, laughing.

"Let's just say, I'm a man of many talents. Milking goats, toting bales, kissing beautiful women in piles of straw."

She stopped in front of him. "You don't think this is strange, do you? I just met you yesterday. I don't really even know you and we've been…intimate. And it doesn't bother me."

"Sometimes it just happens like that," he said. "Fate."

"Has it ever happened to you? Because it's never happened to me."

"No," Dermot replied. "This would be the first time."

"It's like we already knew each other. We didn't start from the beginning, we started in the middle."

He bent close and kissed her. "I just know how I feel. And this feels…just right."

She pushed up on her toes and kissed him back, then frowned. "Did you get breakfast this morning? We didn't have dinner last night, did we? When did you last eat?"

"I had your burned cherry pie in the middle of the night and I had cereal for breakfast."

"I've been doing a terrible job of feeding you," Rachel said.

"I'm not starving," he replied. "In fact, I'm perfectly satisfied at the moment."

"We really should get to know each other a little better," she said, walking backward, the blanket swinging from her hand.

Her pale hair was loose and blew in the breeze. Dermot's breath caught as he watched her. He'd never seen a more beautiful creature. Everything about her was designed just for his eyes. "Then tell me something I don't know."

"I played the saxophone in the high school band," she said. "And I was pretty good. Except I hated marching at the football games."

Dermot chuckled. "Really? I would have never guessed. Tell me something else."

"I was the president of my 4-H club. And it wasn't just all about goats. I won grand prize at the county fair for a quilt I made and for my strawberry preserves."

Dermot chuckled. She really was a farm girl at heart. After only a day, he'd come to appreciate the simplicity of life at Clover Meadow. There was no racing from place to place, no people to see or phone calls to take. It was a quiet life, though the burden of responsibility was greater. He sold boats for lots of money. She cared for sixty-some living creatures.

"Now you have to tell me something," Rachel said.

"I'd rather hear more about you."

"No fair."

"All right. I broke my arm falling out of a tree when I was thirteen."

"What were you doing in the tree?"

"My twin brother dared me to climb to the very top. We did a lot of that when we were kids. Dares and double dares and triple dares. I was almost down and then I slipped and fell."

"You have a twin brother?"

Dermot nodded. "Kieran. We're almost identical twins. We do look a lot alike, except I'm much more handsome."

She sighed softly. "I wish I were closer to my siblings. We've just never really known each other. I have two nieces who are older than me. And when I was young I had an imaginary friend named Rosalie. We were going to open a bakery together when we grew up."

Rachel returned to his side, slipping her arm around his as she chatted about her childhood on the farm. Though it sounded idyllic, there was an undercurrent of loneliness in her stories. She never spoke of friends or parties or adventures. Every story was one of solitude.

"You sound like you loved the farm," he said. "Was it difficult to leave for college?"

Rachel nodded. "I was ready to see a little bit of the world. And going to art school was my dream. I was only an hour away and I came home every other weekend. My parents were older and they needed my help."

"And then you left after college?"

"I met a boy. His job took him to San Francisco and I had to make a choice. I thought it was right, but then it wasn't. And then I met another man and we moved to New York and that didn't work either." She smiled. "I don't have a very good history with men."

"They were both idiots," he said. "Tell me about these greeting cards that you make."

"I don't actually make them. I'm an illustrator. I provide the art and a publisher makes and sells them. It started with farm animals and silly puns. You know, like 'Thinking of Ewe' with an illustration of a sheep. *E-W-E*. You? They're kind of whimsical and people just really liked them. They provide a nice living, although goat farming doesn't allow much time for art."

"Now that I'm here, that will change."

As they walked out past the goat pastures, the landscape began to change. Rolling hills gave way to wooded areas and they followed a ridge, then walked through a wide field to a small grove of trees. To

Dermot's surprise, there was a wide creek running through the trees.

It was one of the most picturesque spots he'd ever seen, the water, the lush green trees and the blue sky above. "It's like heaven," he said. "When I'm out on the water, I think that it's the most perfect place in the world. But you're right, this is pretty perfect, too. I don't see how you could let this go."

"I know. I'm afraid if I do let it go, I won't have anything left. This is really all I have for a home. Eddie and this farm. My sister and brothers don't know me. At least when I'm here, I feel like I belong. And what would Eddie do? He's lived here his whole life."

"You wouldn't have to be lonely."

She shrugged. "You found me. I guess if I decide to stay, then I have to hope that someone else will find me, too." Drawing a deep breath, she forced a smile. "So this is it," she said. "I used to come here to draw when I was a kid."

He glanced around. She was right. It was a scene out of a landscape painting—the tall trees, an old stone fence, a slow-moving creek. There were birds everywhere, singing from the boughs, and butterflies fluttered on the soft breeze. "I can see why you like it," he said.

"Tell me about your favorite place," she asked as she laid the blanket out on the ground.

He dropped the basket on the center of the blanket and sat down next to her. "I have way too many," he said. "But they're all someplace that can only be appreciated from the cockpit of my sailboat."

"I've never been on a sailboat," she said.

"Now, that's a shame. Maybe we'll have to do something about that."

"Unfortunately, we don't have any oceans around here."

"You do have an awfully big lake not too far away. Maybe I'll take you someday." In truth, he wasn't sure how that was going to happen. He had no money to rent a boat and no car to drive them there. He could barely afford to take her for ice cream at this point.

She opened the picnic basket and pulled out a sketchbook and pencil. Then she stared out at the scene in front of her.

"Can I see your drawings?" Dermot asked.

She handed him the book and he flipped through the pages. There were all sorts of wild animals—squirrels, rabbits, porcupines. They looked very realistic except for their funny faces. Dermot chuckled. "These are really good," he said.

"I'm working on some little reptiles and amphibians," she said. "And insects." She reached over and turned to a drawing of a bee. "I think they'll do pretty well. I met this publisher at a convention once and she told me I should be illustrating children's books."

"Do you ever draw people?"

"I used to, in art school." She frowned. "I'm not

sure if I can anymore." She grabbed the book and set it on her lap. "Take your shirt off. And lie down. I'll try drawing you."

"I'm not sure I want to be on your new series of nude-men greeting cards."

Rachel grinned. "That's a good idea. I wonder if there'd be a market for them. Maybe mail order, but you couldn't put them in a grocery store or a gift shop. Maybe an X-rated gift shop." She frowned. "I'm not sure I'd want my cards sold next to dildos and vibrators, though."

Dermot stretched out at the end of the blanket. "How's this?"

She shook her head. "No, sit up and brace your arm right there."

He did as he was told, but she shook her head again. "It would be better if you stood next to that rock over there."

Dermot gave her a sly look. "Maybe it would be even better if I took my clothes off."

"You'll use any excuse to get naked," she said. "But I think that might be a bit distracting for the artist. You can take your shoes off. I need practice with feet."

He kicked off his shoes, then walked over to the rock and leaned against it. "How's this?"

She tipped her head to the side. "Nice. Put your arms up over your head. And undo the top button of your jeans." Rachel waited for him to comply, then began to sketch, her forehead creased into a frown.

Dermot stood perfectly still until his calf began to cramp and a bee started buzzing near his crotch. When he felt something slither across his foot, he jumped back. "Jaysus, what was that? Are there snakes around here?"

"Yes," she said as she sketched. "But they're not poisonous." She sat back, then shook her head. "Nope." With that, she tore the page out of the book and crumpled it into a ball.

"Wait, let me see."

"No," she said, grabbing the wad of paper. "I need to stick to animals."

He sat down next to her and held out his hand. "Come on, Rachel. You can trust me. Let me see it."

RACHEL WAS ALWAYS rather reluctant to let anyone see a work in progress, but she sensed that she could trust Dermot. She handed him the paper and he smoothed it out on the blanket in front of him. He studied it for a long moment, then nodded. "It's really good."

"It's really horrible. The drawing, not you. You looked beautiful. I think I'll stick to bunnies and frogs."

He reached over and wrapped his hand around her waist, then pulled her into a kiss. "I can get behind that. I'd rather you didn't start sketching naked men."

"You weren't naked," she said.

"I can remedy that."

"No," she said, a playful smile touching her lips. "I'll take care of it." She reached for the hem of her dress and pulled it over her head. "Now, you sketch me. I showed you my drawing, now you show me yours."

"I can't draw," he said. "My brother Cam, now, he can draw."

She stretched out on the blanket beside him, bracing her head in her hand. The sun filtered through the leaves in the trees and felt warm on her bare skin. She smiled to herself.

There were times when, as a teenager, Rachel would come to this spot and put aside her sketchbook. She'd turn her thoughts to boys, to the secret crushes that she developed on classmates. She'd been an awkward girl with plain clothes, not the type that got noticed. A wallflower was the most apt description.

"I had my first kiss right here in this spot," she said.

"Tell me all about it," Dermot urged.

"I told a boy I liked that I'd found a huge piece of gold buried beneath this tree and I'd split the money for it if he'd help me carry it out. And then, when I got him here, I tried to kiss him."

"What happened?"

"He hit me with a stick and told me I was as ugly as a toad. And then he ran away."

"I'm not running," Dermot said.

"You're paid to stay," she countered.

He set down the sketchbook and crawled across the blanket. "I'm not planning on going anywhere," he said. "I'm not going to hit you with a stick and I think you're just about the most beautiful thing I've ever set eyes on."

Rachel smiled and pulled him into a deep kiss. He was charming and maybe he did know exactly what to say that made her feel like the only woman in the world. But she didn't care. She'd been alone for too long and she was going to enjoy Dermot Quinn while she could.

Rachel pulled him down on top of her, their naked bodies coming together in a way that felt so perfect. His shaft was hard and hot between them, nestled in the juncture of her thighs. And here, alone, under the late-summer sun, she'd make a memory that she'd never forget. A memory of being with a stranger who felt more like a long-lost lover.

"Are we going to do this?" he whispered.

She drew her leg up along his hip, his body fitting ever closer. "We're alone and we're naked. It is the next logical step."

"I came prepared," he said.

Rachel brushed her lips against his and he captured her mouth in a long, delicious kiss. She'd never been with a man who was able to dissolve her insecurities and inhibitions. Was it the fact that they really didn't know each other? Did that make it all so much easier?

There were no expectations between them, no arguments or fundamental differences. She didn't know anything about his past, about the women in his life or his plans for the future. All Rachel knew was that in six weeks he'd be gone and she'd be alone again.

His body was hard and muscular and she couldn't keep herself from touching him. Dermot held on to her waist and rolled her over on top of him, then pulled her knees up against his hips. A lazy smile curled his lips as he cupped her breast in his palm.

"I've never done this," he said.

"Had sex?"

"No. Done it outside. I mean, I have done it in a tent, but never in the great wide open. What if someone comes along?"

"They'll get an eyeful," she said.

"I'll be sure to make it good."

He began a gentle, yet deliberate exploration of her body and Rachel closed her eyes and enjoyed the sensation of his caress. He knew exactly what he was doing, tracing a path from her lips to her breasts to the spot between her legs.

She was already damp with desire, and when he touched her there, a current shot through her body. Goose bumps prickled her sun-warmed skin and she felt a tremble inside her. She was already so close, but she didn't want to surrender quite yet.

Rachel reached down and touched her lips to his, teasing him with a kiss that was both playful and filled with promise. Her tongue flicked across his bottom lip, and when he groaned, she smiled.

She'd never felt in control before, never felt as if she had anything to offer a man sexually, besides her body. But with Dermot, it all seemed so natural and in balance. He wanted her as much as she wanted him.

Rachel knew everything would change once they took this last step. Though their high-speed affair had taken an unconventional path, from now on, they'd know each other intimately. She'd be completely vulnerable to her feelings, to the effect he had on her body and her soul.

When he reached for his jeans, she knew what he wanted and she impatiently grabbed the packet from his hand. Waving it at him, she smiled. "You did come prepared."

"I've been prepared since the first time we kissed," he said.

"You knew this would happen?"

"I knew what I wanted. But I didn't know that you'd want it, too."

She tore open the condom package and gently sheathed him, smoothing her hands along the length of his shaft. Then, she positioned herself above him and held her breath as she slowly sank down.

The sensation of him inside her, buried deep, was almost more than she could bear. A gasp slipped from her lips and she felt the tension within her heighten at the thought of what they were about to do. She moved above him, and before she knew it, they'd begun a slow, steady rhythm.

Her mind focused on the spot where they were joined, and when he touched her there, Rachel knew how it all would end. Her pulse quickened along with her pace and he continued to tease her, each flick of his finger sending wild sensations coursing through her.

Her hair tumbled around her face and she tipped her head back and closed her eyes. The breeze warmed her skin and the leaves rustled above her head. There was no place on earth she'd rather be.

She looked down at him and smiled, smoothing her hands over his chest. Her lips found his nipple and she sucked gently, teasing at it until it was hard. There was so much to love about his body, so many tempting places to explore.

But he brought her back to her own release when he touched her again. Rachel groaned softly, her eyes going wide as the first shudder consumed her. As if he were waiting for that first sign, Dermot drove deep, and like a wave crashing over her head, her body dissolved into deep and shattering spasms.

For a long moment, every nerve in her body tingled and every synapse in her brain fired. Shudders rocked her, and in the midst of it all, Dermot came, losing himself while buried deep inside her.

Their orgasms melded into one perfect release, and when they were both spent, he pulled her down on top of him and held her close. Rachel rested against his chest, listening to his heart as it slowed to normal again.

Dermot furrowed his fingers through her hair and kissed the top of her head. "I guess it's true what they say about farmers' daughters," he murmured.

"Oh, it gets much better than this," Rachel said.

"How is that possible?" he asked, drawing back to look into her eyes.

"The county fair starts next weekend. There are rides and cream puffs and corn dogs."

"Is there a place for us to do this?"

"No," she said. "But there are pig races, which for some folks around here is better than sex."

He pushed up on his elbow. "Pig races? Really. Isn't it kind of hard to ride a pig?"

Rachel giggled. "No, people don't ride the pigs. The pigs just run around a track."

"That would never be better than sex with you," he said.

"I promise to show you a really good time." At that moment, she was ready to promise Dermot anything. She was blissfully happy with life on the farm, and the way she looked at it, life would only get better.

4

THE GOATS FROM Clover Meadow Farm were one of the biggest attractions at the county fair. Dermot and Rachel delivered six nannies and three kids safely to a pen designed by the local 4-H group and staffed by friendly high school students.

Dermot leaned up against the fence and watched as Rachel spoke with a young boy, showing him how to feed one of the kids a handful of corn. She smiled and laughed as the goat nudged the little boy's hip, looking for more treats in his pocket.

They'd been together for just over a week and his desire for her hadn't cooled. After their first time at the creek, they'd indulged at least once a day, sometimes twice, finding a private hour or two outside of the workday.

Either Uncle Eddie had been too distracted to notice what was going on or he didn't care. But Dermot was beginning to think that Eddie might be holding out hopes that Dermot would choose to stay at the end of his six-week term. He'd found more time to train Benny the goat to do little tricks.

Rachel glanced up at him and he winked at her. She looked so pretty, dressed in a pale blue sundress and a wide-brimmed straw hat. He'd come into her world here at the fair, a world that he was completely unfamiliar with, and he'd seen the respect the children and teenagers had for her.

Rachel wasn't the typical farmer. In truth, she was probably a role model for many of the girls, a single woman trying to make it on a farm all by herself. One of the girls walked over to her and Rachel put an arm around her as they spoke. She laughed and Dermot smiled to himself. She was the prettiest woman at the fair, that much was certain.

"So, I'm done here," she said. "We have the rest of the afternoon to ourselves. What would you like to see first?"

"I've kind of liked watching you," he said, taking hold of her hand. "You're pretty amazing."

"Thanks," she said. "But you see me every day. I think we should start with food. Funnel cakes first, then cream puffs."

"What is a funnel cake?"

"You'll see," she said. She unlatched the gate on the pen and slipped out, one of the goats nipping at her skirt as she left.

They walked hand in hand down a long aisle of

food trucks. There was fresh lemonade and deep-fried cheese and corn dogs and cotton candy. Every trailer they passed had something that Dermot wanted to eat. When they reached the stand for the funnel cakes, he looked at the picture and wrinkled his nose.

"What is this?"

"It's really good," she said. "You'll like it, I promise."

"It looks like a pile of poo. What are you going to make me eat?"

"It's deep-fried batter. Kind of like a donut only shaped like a little mountain. And they cover it with powdered sugar and you eat it while it's—"

"I think we need to go back to that place with the deep-fried cheese. I've developed a real fondness for cheese."

Rachel ordered a funnel cake, then held it out to him. Dermot reluctantly took a bite. The dough was hot and crispy and it melted in his mouth. "Oh, God, that's, like, the best thing I've ever tasted."

She looked at him and giggled. "You have powdered sugar all over your face."

"Do I?" Dermot grinned. "Kiss it off."

Rachel grabbed a napkin and wiped his face. "You behave yourself," she warned. "Or I'll have to take you home early and put you to bed."

They sat down on a picnic table on one of the covered patios and continued to pick at the funnel cake. "I found something that I want to show you," he said.

Rachel glanced over at him. "What is it?"

"An idea. I know it's really not my place, but I'll just mention it and you can do what you want with it."

She watched him warily. "All right. What is it?"

He reached into his pocket and withdrew the bar of soap, setting it in front of her. "This is goat's milk soap. They're selling these at a booth for five dollars a bar. They make the soap with pretty ordinary ingredients. It's not difficult. You could do it in your kitchen."

"You want me to make soap?"

"Not necessarily. I think you could market soap. It could bring in some extra money for the farm. Maybe make things a little easier."

"What's the difference between selling it and marketing it?"

"The soap could be made somewhere else. But you could design the packaging and then market it to natural-food stores and bath boutiques using the farm's name. It's really all about the packaging and you could do a nice job with that." He shrugged. "I guess, if you're interested, I could do some research for you. See if it would be profitable?"

She stared down at the bar of soap, turning it over and over in her hands. "I—I don't know. It is a really good idea. I—I just don't know if it's right…for me."

"I just thought if you were going to stay, this might be something that…" He forced a smile, then reached out and took her hand. "I want to help you, Rachel. I want you to be happy."

Rachel nodded, then stood, smoothing her hands over her skirt. "I think we should see a little more of the fair."

Dermot tried to read her mood. She seemed open to his suggestion, but at the same time, she looked sad…or worried. He wasn't sure which. It wouldn't have to mean more work for her. Maybe he hadn't explained it the right way.

Her mood lightened as they ate their way up one side and down the other side of the food area. By the time they finished, Dermot was stuffed. Though he enjoyed fine dining in some of Seattle's best restaurants, he had to admit that this was one of the best meals he'd ever eaten. Considering the company, he wasn't surprised.

"Exhibits next or rides?" Rachel asked.

"Not rides," he said. "I need to give myself some time to digest."

She laughed. "I've never seen anyone eat so much."

"I wanted to try everything," he said.

"We haven't even started with the brats and sweet corn yet."

Dermot draped his arm around her shoulders. "What I'd really like is to go home. I'd like to take off all my clothes and turn on the fans and lie down on your bed and spend the rest of the day…digesting. Oh, wait, I meant to say kissing you."

"One more thing," she said, taking his hand.

They finished their day with a ride on the Ferris wheel, enjoying a rare moment of quiet together as they were swept up above the crowd and then back down into the bustle. He wrapped his arm around her shoulder and pulled her close, kissing the top of her head.

"This was a good day," he murmured, Rachel tucked in the crook of his arm.

"It was," she said.

"I think I tasted everything."

"We didn't even get to the baked potatoes. And there are chocolate éclairs and barbecued chicken and grilled cheese sandwiches and—"

Dermot groaned as he put his hand over her mouth. "Stop."

Rachel reached out and patted his belly. "You can work it all off in the barn."

"And in bed," Dermot added.

They got off the Ferris wheel and headed toward the parking area where they'd left the pickup. Dermot held her hand as they walked, uninterested in the displays they passed and intent on getting back to the farm as soon as possible. They passed a booth for solar-heating systems and the guy behind the counter stared at Rachel for a long moment.

"Rachel? Rachel Howe?"

Rachel stopped and turned, frowning at first before a wide smile broke across her face. "Danny! Oh, my gosh. Look at you!"

"Look at you," he said.

The man stepped from behind the counter and held out his arms. Dermot felt a surge of jealousy and watched warily as they greeted each other.

"What are you doing here?"

"Business," he said. "I've got a solar-heating and wind-power operation I run out of Janesville." He grabbed a brochure and handed it to her.

Rachel flipped through it, nodding approvingly. "Gosh, I haven't seen you since high school."

"I barely recognized you. I wouldn't have except for that smile. I could never forget that smile. Are you back for a visit?"

"I'm running my parents' farm now. We've got our goats over at the 4-H petting zoo." She turned to Dermot. "This is my—my friend Dermot Quinn. He works at the farm. He's visiting from Seattle."

Danny held out his hand. "Danny Mathison," he said, introducing himself. "Seattle. Great city. I've been there a couple of times."

"Nice to meet you," Dermot said, trying to sound friendly. He didn't like the way Danny was looking at Rachel.

Danny quickly turned his attention back to her. "So, you're living in the area. That's good. And you're still single?"

"Yes," she said, a pretty blush staining her cheeks.

"Me, too. Hey, we should get together some night. Get some dinner and maybe catch a movie. Maybe play a little saxophone?"

"That would be great," Rachel said with a laugh. "Everything except for the saxophone."

"Then I'll give you a call," he said. Danny leaned close and kissed her cheek. "It was really great seeing you again. You're in the book?"

"Right where I've always been," she said.

"Good." He grinned. "Great."

Rachel said goodbye and she and Dermot continued on toward the parking lot. "'That would be great'?" Dermot parroted. "'Hey, we should get together some night.' You know what he meant, don't you? We should get together?"

"I think he wants to go out for dinner and a movie," Rachel said.

"No, that's not what he's got on his mind. He's thinking you're all alone on the farm and he's going to swoop in and show you a good time and he's going to get some."

Rachel laughed out loud. "Get some? Like you've been getting some?"

"No, not like that. With us, it's a mutual thing."

"And what makes you think it wouldn't be a mutual thing with him?" Rachel asked, her eyebrow cocked up quizzically.

"So you want to go out with him?"

"Maybe. He's an old friend, he's kind of cute and

he's got a good job. And he is geographically available, unlike you."

"I'm here."

"But you won't be in another month," she said. "Am I supposed to live like a nun after you leave?"

"Yes," Dermot said. "That would be exactly how you should live."

"You're jealous," she said.

"Damn right I am."

Rachel shook her head. "You don't have to be. I'm not going to go out with Danny. I'm kind of having a little fling with this farmhand. And he takes up all my time and energy."

Dermot grinned. "All right. That's better. And what was that stuff about playing the saxophone? What did he mean by that?"

"We used to sit next to each other in band," Rachel explained. She slipped her arm around his. "Gosh, I went an entire year without a single guy even noticing me and now I've got two interested. I don't know what to do with myself."

DARK CLOUDS ROLLED IN right after breakfast, and the rain came down in sheets. Rachel had hoped to bale hay now that she had someone to work the wagon. But with the rain, it would be at least another week before the cut alfalfa would be dry enough to bale.

Dermot had been out in the barn, trying to repair a broken gate, and she'd been tempted to join him.

But they'd spent so much time together that she was beginning to find it hard to think about anything but him.

He'd been at the farm for three weeks and yet it seemed as if they'd already spent a lifetime together. She'd grown so accustomed to having him around, grown to depend on him when things seemed to get impossible.

But if the days were good, the nights were even better. Once the sun went down, they lived in a sexy, delicious dream in which Dermot Quinn turned her into a wild, wanton woman. A month ago, she'd fantasized about a man who'd pull her into his arms and kiss her without a second thought, but never, in all her dreams had she actually expected it to happen.

And though the sex wasn't strange or kinky, it was powerfully addictive. When he touched her, there was always an earth-shattering reaction. She wanted him to brush aside her clothes and kiss her naked skin, to pull her to the bed and seduce her until she trembled at his touch. Until desire bubbled up inside of her and she begged him to continue. Until she was completely and utterly spent, rid of every last bit of need.

How could she possibly live without him? She stared down at her accounting book, then slammed it shut. Why couldn't she just enjoy Dermot while he was here? Why did her thoughts always turn to the future?

"Forget it," she muttered. The last thing she needed

in her life was another complication. Though sleeping with Dermot was very pleasant and more than satisfying, it wouldn't be wise to succumb to such a powerful addiction. She'd just have to keep her emotions in check. Falling in love with him would be the biggest mistake she could ever make.

Rachel reached out and grabbed the recipe for goat's milk soap that Dermot had found on the internet. She stared at it for a long moment. He'd gone out and purchased all the ingredients, but left it to her to decide what she wanted to do.

She pushed back from the table and found her sketch pad on the counter. Her box of colored pencils sat next to it and she retrieved them both, then sat back down. She ought to work on her greeting cards, since she'd fallen behind on the publisher's schedule. But she'd been toying with an idea for a label, yet was reluctant to put it to paper.

Was it worth the time? She hadn't even decided to stay on the farm and this was a project that would require a complete commitment to a future at Clover Meadow. But then, doing a drawing wasn't exactly going to cost her anything.

She bent over her sketchbook and began, focusing on the perfect balance of text, graphics and illustration. She wasn't aware of the time, but when she was finished, she glanced up at the clock. She'd done the entire label in less than fifteen minutes.

"Nice," she murmured.

Rachel found a bar of hand soap under the sink and wrapped the new label around it. Her parents would have loved the idea. Her mother might have enjoyed making the soap herself and her father would have been tickled to know that goat's milk could be used in a new way.

The screen door squeaked and she glanced over her shoulder to see Dermot standing in the doorway. He was soaking wet, water dripping off his hair and puddling around his muddy boots.

"If you're going to come in the house, you have to take off your clothes on the porch," she warned. "I just washed the floor."

"I can do that," he said, tugging off his T-shirt and tossing it aside. Bracing his arm on the doorjamb, he kicked off his boots, then moved to unbutton his jeans.

Rachel watched him, her gaze skimming over his broad shoulders and finely muscled chest. He was the most beautiful man, his body made for the kind of work he did on the farm. Over the past three weeks, his skin had been burnished brown by the sun.

"Are you sure you don't want to do this?" he asked.

"I like watching," she said.

When he was down to his blue cotton boxers, he stepped inside. Hooking his thumbs in the waistband, he slowly pushed them down over his hips. When they dropped to the floor, Rachel's breath caught in her throat. Dermot walked across the kitchen in all his naked glory, a devilish smile on his face, then pulled her into his arms.

"Now that you have me naked, what are you going to do with me?" he murmured, his warm breath soft on her neck.

Rachel ran her hands over his slick skin. "You're cold," she said.

"Warm me up."

She took his hand and led him through the house and up the stairs. He turned toward her bedroom, but she pulled him into the bathroom. She turned on the faucets and began to fill the huge claw-foot tub.

"Are we having a bath?" he asked.

"Yes. You are."

"Are you going to join me?"

"No," she said. "But I will wash your back."

When the tub was half-full, he stepped in and sat down. Rachel grabbed a washcloth from the basket next to the tub and dipped it in the water. She'd studied his body so intently over the past few weeks that she knew every inch of skin from the tiny birthmark on his shoulder to the crooked scar on his knee.

She'd never taken the time to know a man quite so intimately. Rachel was left to wonder if he'd be the last man in her life. If she decided to stay on the farm, she knew her future might be spent in solitude. She bit at her bottom lip. Since Dermot had arrived, the choice to stay had become even more difficult to fathom.

Her promises to her father were made in a desperate moment, when he needed comfort and reassurance. But there came a point when she had to live her own life. And what if that life couldn't be lived here on the farm?

"Are you all right?"

"Fine," she croaked. This would be one of those moments that she remembered forever, she mused. Every one of her senses was so finely tuned that the memory was imprinted on her soul. She reached out and brushed the damp hair out of his eyes.

Dermot leaned over the edge of the tub and cupped her cheek in his hand. A moment later, Rachel was caught inside a long, lingering kiss, one that made her head spin and her body tremble.

She wanted to stop him, but she'd lost any sense of who or what she was. Every ounce of her attention was focused on the taste of his mouth, the feel of his lips against hers.

When he finally drew away, he met her gaze. Rachel forced a smile, then went back to washing his back, but he grabbed her hand. "What's wrong?"

"Nothing," she said. "It's just a gray day. And I've got a lot on my mind."

"Tell me."

Rachel shook her head. "It's nothing." She paused, then drew a deep breath and let it out. "I'm just trying to figure out my future and you keep getting in the way. Not that I don't love having you here, because I do. But it just makes everything so much more difficult."

"I don't want to do that," Dermot said.

"I know. But so much of my happiness right now is because I'm…you know."

"Well satisfied?"

"Yes, that, too. But I was going to say *relaxed*. Less worried. The list of things that need doing on the farm is getting shorter and shorter every day. And it makes a life here more attractive. Which makes my decision more difficult."

"So, what do you want me to do? We could spend more time in bed and less time working."

"I hired you to work, not to…pleasure me."

"I can multitask. I'm very good at that."

Rachel smiled, well aware of his abilities both inside and outside the bedroom. "I just think that it's going to take me a lot longer to figure this out."

"I think it would help if you'd take your clothes off and get in the tub with me. A hot bath always helps me focus."

"You take baths?"

Dermot shook his head. "No. Never. But I'll say just about anything to get you in the tub with me." He grabbed her hand and pressed a kiss to the center of her palm. "Come on. You'll see."

Rachel slowly undressed, then stepped into the tub and settled herself against his chest. He took the washcloth and sloshed water over her breasts and shoulders and she closed her eyes and relaxed into the warmth of his body.

"Let's talk about your choices," he said. "You can stay and run the farm."

"Mmm-hmm."

"Or you can sell it," he continued.

"Those are my only two choices."

"Could you lease it out? Find someone else to run it until you're ready to make a decision."

"I never really thought about that. My sister and brothers want to settle the estate. They want it sold."

"All right. Would it make you feel better if you got the right kind of people to buy it? Maybe find a family who wants to continue the same type of work your father did? Would that help?"

"Yes," she said. Rachel thought about the notion for a long moment. "A family, with kids, who want to raise goats and show them at the fair. With a mother who likes to garden and a father who wants to work for himself. This farm works best for a family."

"Then maybe we need to find a family like that," he said. "Can you think of anyone that you know?"

Rachel closed her eyes again and Dermot wrapped his arms more tightly around her. There were plenty of family farms in the area, but they were all struggling. Still, if she could offer a family a stable income, there would be buyers.

"I'm so lucky you came into my life," Rachel said.

She turned over and smoothed her hands over his chest, pressing a kiss to his damp skin.

Dermot kissed the top of her head. "I think I was the lucky one."

"When you first met me, how long did it take before you knew you wanted to sleep with me?"

He smiled, nuzzling her temple. "I think it was about six or seven...seconds. I went through all the pros and cons on the ride to the farm. And then there was that kiss and it was game on from there. Since then, I can't seem to stop myself."

"Do you ever wonder if it might have been a mistake?"

He shook his head. "How could anything that feels so good be a mistake?" He laughed. "Are you really thinking it was?"

"Do you know what today is?"

"Wednesday?"

"You've been on the farm for exactly three weeks. That means that your time here is half over. In three weeks, you have to go home."

His grin faded. "Really? It seems like I just got here. I don't want to think about leaving."

Rachel shrugged. "When you walked up to my truck, I thought you'd dropped out of the sky, like an answer to my prayers. But the longer you stay, the harder it will be to let you go."

"I know," he said. He kissed her again. "I know."

As the water in the tub began to cool, Rachel knew

they ought to get out. It was a perfect metaphor for the relationship. How long could they continue before it became impossible to let go? She was coming perilously close to the point of no return, to the point where his leaving would cause permanent heartache and unresolved regrets.

She wasn't in love yet, but everything pointed in that direction. Dermot Quinn was a man well worth loving. And if she didn't take that step, then another woman in another place and another life would. And he would be lost to her forever.

THE HEAT OF THE AFTERNOON was oppressive, the humidity thick in the air. Dermot reached for another bag of feed and hoisted it onto the back of the pickup. Harley and Sam, the two farmers he'd met his first day in Mapleton, sat on the porch of the feed store, watching him from beneath the brims of their caps. A few seconds later, another farmer joined them and they chatted, pointing in his direction.

Dermot sighed softly, then braced his gloved hands on his hips and turned toward them. "If you boys have any questions I can answer, just let me know."

They seemed shocked that he'd called them out. "Nope. No questions," Sam said.

"No?" Dermot asked, walking toward them. "I can see something is worrying you. Just spit it out."

"We were just speculating on how much longer

Miss Rachel was going to last on that farm," Sam finally said.

"What difference does it make to you?"

"She's got a nice piece of land there," Harley told him. "And there are folks that are interested in having that land for themselves. In fact, there's probably going to be quite a little bidding war if she ever decides to sell."

"Well, she's not going to sell," Dermot said. "So you can let all those interested folks know that they can stop being interested and find themselves something else to do with their time."

"Seems like you've made yourself very…comfortable over at Clover Meadow," Harley observed. "We're all taking bets on how long you'll be staying."

"Who knows?" Dermot said. "Maybe I'm not going to leave at all."

He strode back to the pallet on the loading dock and tossed the last three bags of feed into the truck, then jumped down and got behind the wheel. He had dropped Rachel at the post office and they planned to do the grocery shopping after that. But Dermot was beginning to feel that this small town was just a little too small for him.

Maybe it was natural that people were curious about what was going on at Clover Meadow Farm, but he still didn't care for anyone drawing conclusions about his relationship with Rachel. Yet why should it make him angry? Dermot cursed beneath his breath.

She'd have to live here after he was gone. People would talk, and gossip was never good for a woman's reputation. Hell, he'd been the one to put all that at risk. Maybe she would have been better off with that Danny guy from the county fair. At least he was geographically available.

Dermot steered the truck toward the main street of Mapleton, his mind going through everything that had happened between Rachel and him. It had seemed so simple that day they met. They were both adults, both curious about the attraction between them, both willing and able. But in retrospect, Dermot hadn't thought beyond the initial gratification.

If he really cared, then he wouldn't have been so cavalier about moving into her bedroom. He pulled the truck to a stop in front of the post office and waited, peering at the front door through the passenger window. A pair of older women passed by on the sidewalk, and when they saw him, they immediately turned to each other and began talking.

Frustrated, Dermot pressed on the horn, startling the old biddies and sending them scurrying. A few seconds later, Rachel emerged. She ran down the front steps and he reached over to open the passenger side door. She settled herself in the seat beside him.

"We need to talk," he muttered.

"This is from some lawyer that my brothers have hired." She held up the envelope. "Registered mail. They want to have me removed as executor of my father's estate. They're saying I exerted undue influence on him when he wrote his will. They want to force me to sell the farm."

Dermot gasped. "Jaysus, Rachel. Can they do that?"

"I—I don't know. I can't afford to hire a lawyer to find out. Do they think I wanted this? He made me promise, on his deathbed. I love the farm, but I don't know if I want to spend my life there." She covered her face with her hands. "Maybe I should just sell. It's three against two. Eddie and I are the only ones who want to keep the farm in the family."

He reached over and pulled her into his arms, then noticed the people standing on the street watching them. With a soft curse, he turned the ignition and started the truck.

Once he got out of town, Dermot followed the signs for a small county park that they'd passed a number of times. He headed down a quiet tree-lined drive and pulled the truck off into a parking lot, overlooking a picnic shelter. Reaching for Rachel, he drew her into his embrace.

When the tears suddenly came pouring out, he wasn't sure what to do. Hell, he wasn't really sure why she was crying. Was it because of the letter from the lawyer, or was she just so tired that anything would put her over the edge?

He stroked her back and whispered to her, softly telling her what he thought she needed to hear. When she finally quieted, he drew back and looked down into her watery eyes. "It's going to be all right," Dermot murmured. "We'll figure this out, I promise."

His hands lingered on her hips as his gaze fell to her mouth. Sniffling, Rachel leaned forward and touched her lips to his. "Thank you," she said.

"For what?"

"For being the only one that seems to care about what I want."

"Sweetheart, that will never change. No matter what happens, you can always count on me."

She nodded. "How is it that you're still single? Why hasn't some woman married you and made you an honest man?"

"I don't know," Dermot said. "Maybe I just haven't met the right woman yet."

"When you do, she's going to be very lucky."

Dermot slipped his hands around her waist and pulled her body against his. He took his time, focusing on the feel of her lips beneath his, waiting for the silent cues to her need. His lips touched her left eyelid and then her right, kissing away the tears. "Tell me this makes you feel better."

She sighed deeply as he kissed her temple. "Yes," Rachel said. "It feels good."

He hooked his finger beneath her chin and tipped her gaze up to meet his. And then he kissed her again, his tongue teasing at her lips before gently invading her mouth. But this kiss was meant to tempt her, to show her that this wasn't just about desire. Rachel wrapped her arms around his neck and surrendered, and Dermot felt a familiar rush of heat course through his body as he pushed her back against the passenger door.

His hands slid down her waist to her hips, then circled to smooth over her back. How would he ever do without this? He'd come to crave the feel of her in his arms, the taste of her mouth, the scent of her hair. Dermot knew that he ought to step back, to regain his perspective. But everything about her drew him deeper, until he felt as if she were the only lifeline in a whirlpool of unfamiliar emotions.

He slowly eased away, bracing his hands on either side of her body. Was he falling in love? Everything about this woman made him want to protect her. It wasn't about his own pleasure anymore, but about her happiness. And yet, Dermot wasn't even sure he'd know love if it hit him over the head.

He just barely remembered his parents, how they laughed with each other, how they'd share a secret moment when they thought no one was watching. Was that love? Because he had all of that with Rachel.

"You said we needed to talk," Rachel said at last. "About what?"

Dermot shook his head. "Nothing. It was…nothing."

Rachel grabbed the front of his shirt and pulled him back down on top of her. She reached for the buttons of his work shirt, dropping kisses on each bit of exposed flesh.

There were moments when they couldn't seem to get close enough. His hand moved to her breast and she moaned softly. Dermot grazed his thumb across her nipple. He watched as she arched against his touch, her breath coming in quick gasps and her lips damp.

He had three weeks left with Rachel, three weeks to figure out why she meant so much to him. Would it be enough? Or would he be forced to walk away without ever really knowing if they belonged together? There were so many questions that needed to be answered already, and the list just kept getting longer.

5

It was a perfect summer night. The sky was clear, the sunset turning the western horizon orange and pink. Rachel stood at the screen door, staring out into the quiet yard. The first crickets had started to chirp, a pretty counterpoint to the sound of the baseball game coming from the truck radio.

Dermot sat on the porch steps, tossing a little ball into the yard for Benny, who danced around it playfully before picking it up in his mouth and carrying it back to Dermot.

It was a testimony to how easily Dermot had found his place on the farm and a special connection with the animals. Benny usually did whatever he wanted, causing as much trouble as he could along the way. But now he seemed to be content to play a goat version of "fetch," a brand-new trick for him.

She pushed open the screen door and it squeaked. Dermot glanced over his shoulder. "Mariners are ahead, six to four. And I didn't know goats could fetch."

"Neither did I. He's never done that before."

"Really?"

Rachel nodded. "Do you go to baseball games when you're at home?" she asked.

He nodded. "My brothers and I have season tickets. I usually get to at least one game a week when they're in town."

She sat down beside him and wrapped her arms around her knees. "Tell me what you'd be doing if you were home. I want to be able to imagine your life after you've left."

He reached out and caught her chin. "Do you think I'm just going to disappear from your life when my six weeks are up?"

Rachel shrugged. "I—I don't know. I'm not sure what's going to happen. Are you going to disappear?"

"No," he said. "I think we'll talk. And maybe you could come to Seattle to visit me. I could take you sailing. Or I could visit the farm. It's not like I'm going to be living on the moon. There are planes that fly back and forth between Chicago and Seattle."

Rachel sighed softly. As much as she needed a vacation, she knew the reality of her situation. "You know how difficult it is for me to get away. The dairy requires me to be here every day of every week."

"Then we're going to have to find someone to help

you out after I leave. And he's going to be old and toothless and preferably gay."

Rachel laughed. "Oh, so you don't want me hanging around the bus stop and hiring another Dermot Quinn?"

"I'm one of a kind. You'll never find another farmhand like me."

She stood up and walked down the steps. "I'm going to get the mail. Do you want to come with me?"

Dermot shook his head. "No, I think I'll just stay here and watch."

As Rachel walked to the driveway, she swayed her hips provocatively and he gave her a wolf whistle. "Work it, baby," he called.

She usually avoided the mail for as long as she could, sometimes letting it build up for a week. It was always the same thing—bills, bills, bills. The power, the feed store, the vet.

She opened the box and pulled out a stack of envelopes, then walked back down the driveway, flipping through them. One piece of mail caught her attention and she pulled it from the bunch, staring at the return address. Minneapolis.

When she reached the porch, she sat down again and waved the envelope at Dermot. "A letter from my sister, Jane," she said.

"Really," he murmured. He grabbed the envelope and examined it. "Are you going to open it?"

"I know what's inside. She's going to try to convince me to sell the farm. I'm sure she could use the money for a new car or a vacation to Mexico. She lives in a neighborhood where money is very, very important."

"Don't open it," Dermot said.

But Rachel didn't want to shy away from the conflict any longer. She felt stronger now, as if she could finally stand up for herself and state her case. Her father had left the decisions about the farm to her. She was the executor of his estate. "I want to see what she has to say."

Rachel ripped open the envelope, pulled out a three-page letter and began to read. But the subject wasn't at all what she'd expected. "Oh. She and her husband are having problems. They're getting a divorce. He took all their money and ran off with… Oh, no. He ran off with another woman."

Dermot slipped his arm around her shoulders, pulling her close. He took the letter from her and continued reading. "She needs time to sort out her life. She wants to send her boys to live on the farm to get them away from all the gossip."

"I don't even know them. I met them six or seven years ago when they came for Christmas when my mom was still alive. They haven't been to the farm since then. They're probably teenagers now." Rachel leaned over to read the rest of the letter. "When does she want to send them?"

"As soon as possible," he said. "She wants you to call her."

A long silence grew between them. How could she refuse? This was the first time any of her siblings had ever asked her for anything—beyond their demands to sell the farm. She wanted to believe she might one day have a relationship with her brothers and sister, but this was not the way she wanted it to happen.

"What are you going to do?" Dermot asked.

"She's family. And she needs my help. I can't say no." She met his gaze and felt a surge of emotion. "What do you think?"

He nodded. "I think you're absolutely right. This will be a good place for your nephews to be while all that turmoil is going on at home. And maybe you and your sister can become a bit closer."

"I've never had many opportunities to deal with teenage boys before," Rachel said. "What if they're naughty?"

"Don't worry. I'll help you out. I was once a teenage boy. I know what's going on in their heads."

Rachel slipped her arms around his neck and kissed him. "Thank you," she murmured.

It was so simple to depend upon him, and yet, she knew that in a few more weeks he'd be gone. Life seemed so much easier when she had Dermot standing in her corner, backing her up, ready to catch her when she fell.

"When they come, they'll have to stay in the house," she said.

"I didn't expect that you'd put them in the barn."

"Which means you're going to have to move back in with Eddie." He opened his mouth to protest, but she put her finger across his lips. "It just wouldn't be right. I have to set a good example. And Jane is very conservative when it comes to her children."

"Well, then, we're going to have to find a place to sneak away every now and then."

Rachel smiled. "I suppose that could be arranged."

"And we're going to have to get in as much sex as we can before they arrive," Dermot added. "Starting now." He stood up and scooped her into his arms, then carried her up the porch steps and into the house.

Maybe this was for the best, Rachel thought. They'd become so close that it was almost impossible to imagine how she could ever let him go. Perhaps by putting some distance between them, the leaving might be a bit less traumatic.

He set her on the edge of the kitchen counter, stepping in between her legs as his hands smoothed up her bare thighs. His lips met hers, and a heartbeat later, they were lost in a deep and stirring kiss.

"I've been thinking about this all day," he said against her mouth, his hands slipping through her hair.

"What were you thinking?" she asked, her breath coming in quick gasps.

"About what would happen once we were alone again."

"We're always alone," she said, unbuttoning his work shirt. "What did you imagine?"

Pushing the soft cotton aside, Rachel reached up and smoothed her hands over his naked chest. "What are we doing here?" she murmured, pressing her lips to his chest.

"I have no idea," Dermot replied, "but I don't want to stop."

He ran his hands down her back and Rachel shivered at the sensation of his touch. "This is going to be impossible," she said, nuzzling her face into his neck.

"We're sleeping in the same bedroom. How is that impossible?"

"How long do you think we can keep this up?" Rachel asked. "It's getting out of control."

Dermot drew her closer, pulled her legs around his waist. She could feel his desire beneath the faded fabric of his jeans. "Out of control is good," he said. "That's exactly how it should be between us."

Rachel reached up to run her fingers along his lower lip. "What do you want from me? Tell me."

"I'm sure we can come up with something." He gently bit at her fingertips. "God, you're beautiful. I've looked at you hundreds of times in the past few weeks and I can't seem to get enough. Not this way."

Dermot tugged the strap of her tank top off her

shoulder and pressed a line of kisses over the gentle curve between her neck and arm.

"I don't know anything about you," she said. "Yet I know you completely."

"It's strange," he said, smoothing his hand across her breast. "But wonderful."

Dermot smiled as he cupped her breast in his hand, teasing at her nipple with his thumb. And then, in one easy motion, he wrapped his arms around her waist and pressed his mouth against her neck. He trailed kisses from her collarbone to her breast, then finally drew the hard nub of her nipple into his mouth. She arched back, holding her breath as he pulled her down into another kiss.

She wanted to tell him how she felt, just blurt it all out and let the consequences fall where they may. What did she have to lose? He was going to leave anyway. Rachel cupped his face in her hands and turned his gaze up to hers. "I'm not sure anymore that I can let you go."

"I'm not sure anymore that I want to leave."

Rachel groaned, tipping her head back and closing her eyes. "Don't say that." She shook her head. "Don't tease me and let me believe you want to stay."

"Why not?"

She opened her eyes and looked at him. "This isn't a game. This is my life."

"What does that mean?" Dermot said, an edge of anger in his voice.

"I think that sometimes you'll say anything to get what you want." Rachel sighed. This conversation was going nowhere. They usually had no trouble communicating, but she couldn't seem to make him understand. "Don't talk about the future like you imagine yourself here."

"Don't you imagine that your life might suddenly become easier?"

"Easier? You think I want you because it makes my life easier?" Though the notion seemed insulting at first, Rachel realized that maybe Dermot was right. Maybe she was falling in love with the idea of a man at Clover Meadow Farm, instead of with the man himself. What did she really know about Dermot, beyond what they shared in the bedroom?

"Are you really that delusional?" Rachel asked. "I don't need you to complete my life. I'm perfectly capable of running this farm on my own."

"Are you?" Dermot asked, his expression intense.

God, was he deliberately provoking her? How had this conversation managed to deteriorate in such a short time. She ought to just walk away, before she said something she couldn't take back. "Yes, I am. In fact, right now, I wish I'd never even hired you. I thought I'd figured out what I wanted and then you came along and screwed it up." She cursed softly. "I was all right being alone. I wasn't happy, but I was fine."

Rachel scrambled off the counter, crossing the

kitchen to stand behind the table, creating a barrier between them. Anger bubbled up inside her. How had she let things go so far? She'd promised herself that she'd protect her heart, and somehow, without even knowing, she'd allowed herself to fall for him.

"I think you should go," she said, humiliated at the emotion that made her voice shake.

"Are you joking?"

"I'll pay you for all six weeks. You'll have enough for a bus ticket home. It would be better for both of us."

"I'm not going anywhere. You hired me to work on this farm for six weeks and that's what I'm going to do. If you don't want me in your bed anymore, that's fine. But I'm not leaving. So you can just forget that."

Rachel cursed softly. Dermot Quinn was stubborn and arrogant. "It's better if we just end it now, before either of us gets in too deep."

His gaze met hers. "I'm not sure that's possible," he replied. "I know it's not possible for me. And I don't think it's possible for you either."

"We need to try." Rachel moved to the door, then turned back to look at him. "I'm going to try."

She yanked open the screen door and walked outside, heading for the barn and a last check on the goats. She felt as if she'd just dodged a terrible danger, her heart slamming in her chest, her adrenaline pumping. It would be easy to fall in love with Dermot and so hard to fall out of love. And right now, she didn't have the strength to fight that battle.

"Send up some more shingles," Dermot called.

He tucked his hammer into the old tool belt and made his way down from the peak of the roof. Eddie was stationed on the ground next to the old stone house, his hands on the rope to a pulley they'd rigged up. As always, Benny was at his side, this time perched on top of a stack of packaged shingles.

Over the past few days, Dermot had worked himself to exhaustion. At first, it helped alleviate his anger. The fight they'd had had been ridiculous. It was clear that Rachel was looking for any excuse to put some space between them and had jumped on the first misunderstanding they'd had.

Once his anger had cooled, he'd used hard work to defuse his sexual energy. It helped to have something to focus on, beyond thoughts of Rachel's lips or her breasts or the way her body felt beneath his.

But now, he needed to drive himself hard just to sleep at night. It was the only way he could deal with the empty spot beside him in bed. If he was tired enough, he could sleep without dreaming of Rachel and her soft skin and naked flesh and— Dermot cursed.

"I'm working as fast as I can," Eddie said. "These things aren't as light as a feather, you know. I'm an old man. Give me a break."

"Sorry," Dermot called down. "I wasn't swearing at you."

Three nights thinking about her, wondering if she was lying awake thinking about him. The days were even worse. He worked beside her in the dairy barn, watching her move, thinking about how nice it would be to drag her into his arms and kiss her until she surrendered again. They ate dinner together, drove to the feed store together, walked out to the pasture to fetch the goats for evening milking.

He understood her reluctance to get close again. They had jumped into the deep end of the desire pool and become expert swimmers in a very short time. Surprising for him since he'd always been rather indifferent about long-term relationships. When the strings came along, he was usually the one to cut and run.

But there were moments when he could actually picture himself living on the farm with Rachel. Those moments occurred at the oddest times—while he was chopping potatoes for dinner or when they were standing at the gate to the goat pen, watching the kids jump and play. This morning it had come when she handed him a mug of coffee.

"Hey, what's goin' on up there?"

Dermot looked over the edge of the roof and waved at Eddie. The package of shingles was nestled inside the bucket and he pulled on the rope.

A few moments later, Eddie appeared at the top of

the ladder. He clambered onto the roof before Dermot had a chance to stop him, nimbly sitting down next to Dermot with a satisfied smile.

"If Rachel catches you up here, she's going to kill me," Dermot warned.

The old man grinned. "At my age, I can do whatever I want. I don't take my orders from her." He paused. "Although it seems that you do."

"I work for her. She's the boss."

"You know what I mean. I can see that something's changed between you. You two used to act like lovesick fools."

"We were not—"

"Don't think I didn't know what was goin' on," Eddie said, wagging his finger at Dermot. "I may be old, but I'm not stupid. There was a spark there, somethin' special. I don't know what happened between you, but whatever it was, I expect the spark is still there."

"We just decided it would be better if—"

"Don't give me that bull. What the hell is better about this? The two of you mopin' around? How is that better?"

Eddie had barely said more than five words to him before this and now he was lecturing him on his relationship with Rachel? This didn't seem real, Dermot mused. But then, Eddie had known Rachel her whole life. Maybe he could offer some valuable advice.

"It's the way Rachel wants it," Dermot said.

"Oh, don't be such a namby-pamby. Take control." Eddie frowned. "I had a spark once. Shoulda married her, but I didn't. Her name was Mary Ellen Duncan. I wasted too much time and some other fella caught her eye and that was the end of it for me. We coulda been happy. We coulda had a good life, but I was too dang polite to tell her how I felt."

"Carpe diem," Dermot murmured.

"What are we talking about now?"

"Carpe diem. It's Latin. Seize the day. But what if I don't know how I feel?" Dermot asked.

Eddie waved his hand dismissively. "Then figure it out. Take off your short pants and be a man. Don't be a mouse. Because, I'll tell you one thing. When she leaves this farm and goes back to the city, there's goin' to be all kinds of men who'll come courting. And I'm not sure you'd be able to stand the competition. You're not that good-lookin'."

"Well, thanks for the advice," Dermot said. "I appreciate it."

Eddie shook his head. "Don't just sit there. Do something about it. Carpe your diem."

"Any suggestions?"

"I suggest you take her out for ice cream. Rachel likes ice cream. Buy her a cone at Ivy's and sit yourself down and have a nice talk. It will do wonders, mark my words."

"Ice cream. All right, I could do that. That's about all I can afford right now."

"Well, do it, then," he said. "Climb down that ladder and make a date. Now. Before you lose your courage."

Dermot groaned, then swung his leg over the ladder. "You better get down before she sees you up here."

"I will," Eddie said, grinning. "You have a good evening, now."

Dermot grabbed his shirt from the porch rail and slipped into it as he crossed the yard. He found her surrounded by goats in the paddock near the milking barn. She held one of the kids in her arms, laughing as he nibbled at her hair.

At first, he was reluctant to interrupt her. She looked so pretty, so happy. She was dressed in a loose cotton sundress, her hair full from the humidity in the air. He clenched his fingers as he thought about the last time he'd touched her, buried his face in her hair, pressed his lips to her neck—he drew a ragged breath—and lost himself in the warmth of her body.

Dermot stood on the lowest rail of the gate and braced his hands on the top edge. "I see I've been replaced," he called.

She turned and looked at him. "Hey."

"I used to be the one who nibbled on your hair. Or have you forgotten already?"

She set the kid down and walked over to the gate. "Are you done for the night?"

He reached out and grabbed her hand. "I am. And

I was wondering if you'd like to drive into town and get some ice cream. It's a beautiful Friday night."

"Are you asking me out on a date?"

"Yeah, maybe I am. Things have been a little tense lately. Would you go out on a date with me?"

She studied him for a long moment then shrugged. "Sure. Let's go."

He opened the gate for her and she stepped out of the pen. Dermot draped his arm around her shoulders as they walked. "What else is there to do in small-town Wisconsin on a Friday night besides watch goats?"

She thought for a long moment. "There's a football game at the high school. And you can usually find a bingo game somewhere in town, at one of the churches or at the fire hall. And the stores on Center Street stay open late. We could go hang out at Meller's Five-and-Dime or Big Jimmy's Hardware."

"All right," he said, "we have choices."

She reached up and grabbed his hand where it rested on her shoulder, giving it a squeeze. "Let's start with the ice cream."

They hopped in the truck and headed off to Mapleton. There was only one place for ice cream, Ivy's Drive-In. Dermot swung the truck beneath the overhang, and a minute later, a carhop put a tag on the windshield and stood next to the driver's door, awaiting their order.

They both ordered a cone, then hopped out of the

truck and walked around to the back. Rachel boosted herself up on the open tailgate, her slender legs dangling.

"I love nights like this," she said. "So warm and so perfect. Makes me wish winter would never come."

"I bet it's beautiful around here in the winter," Dermot said. "I'd like to see it."

She bumped his shoulder. "You would not love the winters here. They're cold and windy. And you don't have to say things like that."

"I'm not supposed to say something I really mean?" He grabbed her hand. "I don't want to argue with you, Rachel. I think we should spend our last few weeks enjoying ourselves."

The carhop appeared with their ice cream cones, defusing the tension between them. Dermot took a bite and smiled. "Raspberry twirl," he said. "Good choice. What did you get?"

"I'm just a vanilla girl," Rachel said.

"You are not vanilla," Dermot said. He leaned close and dropped a kiss on her lips, licking his as he drew back. "Yum."

"That's about as exciting as it's going to get," she teased.

"I like kissing you. I could kiss you all night. Where do people go around here to make out? Maybe we could go see that place."

"I never did that when I was in high school. I was a good girl."

"Well, maybe you should give it a try now."

"And maybe you could take me to the homecoming dance, too," she teased.

"I never went to a high school dance," he said. "That would be fun."

She seemed surprised by his admission. "You never went to a dance? I find that hard to believe."

"Kieran and I really didn't do a whole lot at school. We spent most of our free time working at my grandfather's boatyard. We built a racing sloop junior year of high school, and then senior year, we spent every weekend tearing up and down the sound." He wove his fingers through hers. "Now, if you had gone to our high school, I might have asked you to a dance. Or taken you out on our boat."

"You never would have noticed me," she said. "I used to just blend into the walls. I was very plain and very shy. I was the girl with the pencil case. I used to carry all my colored pencils around in this plastic case with a little handle. It kind of became my thing. I was odd."

"All right. Maybe I wouldn't have asked you out."

She reached over and dabbed a bit of ice cream on the end of his nose. "See. I like it when you're honest with me."

Dermot stared at her for a long moment. He'd been completely honest with her. She was the one who didn't believe him. God, she was the most beautiful, exasperating, exciting woman he'd ever known, and every day that they spent together, she grew more beautiful. He lived for her smile and her laugh and the way her eyes lit up when they spoke.

"Would you like to hear another truth?" he asked.

"First you need to clean the ice cream off the end of your nose."

"You do that," he said.

When she leaned into him, he caught her by surprise, kissing her again. "Here's a truth," he murmured. "I like you a whole lot, Rachel Howe. And if I'm not careful, I might fall in love with you."

Her breath caught in her throat and she stared at him, wide-eyed. "I like you, too," she said.

It felt good to say those words out loud. And he didn't care if all they shared was the occasional kiss from now until he left. He was satisfied just to sit next to her and talk.

He had eighteen days left to figure this all out. It didn't seem like a lot of time, but for the two of them, it would have to be enough.

SLEEP WAS IMPOSSIBLE. Rachel stared at the ceiling of her bedroom and groaned softly. The heat made her skin sticky and her hair damp. Even the fan in the window didn't provide any relief. But she knew it wasn't the heat. It was Dermot.

Her mind was spinning, a tangle of thoughts she just couldn't seem to sort out. She'd left him at the door a few hours before, determined not to let a few delicious kisses rock her resolve to put distance between them.

Was it so difficult for him to understand? She was only trying to protect herself from the hurt that would eventually come. Surely he could see that she was growing far too dependent on him.

It would be so easy to fall in love, to believe that he was some white knight come to rescue her from all her problems. With a partner, she could keep the farm, she could have time to do her work as an artist, she could honor the promise she made to her father. Everything would fall into place so neatly.

But was she idealizing what they shared because she needed him to make her life easier? Or was she feeling a connection that was meant to last a lifetime? Rachel had thought she'd found love in the past and she'd been proved wrong. So what made her think this was the real thing—and after only three weeks together?

With a soft curse, she sat up and raked her hands through her tangled hair. This was crazy! No matter what she did, she was going to get hurt. Even now, the thought of falling asleep without him brought a lonely ache to her heart.

He was a wonderful man, kind and compassionate, patient and concerned, so incredibly sexy. Exactly the sort of man she could see herself loving for the rest of her life. But was she in love or just caught up in the possibility of love?

Her stomach growled. Maybe if she made herself a snack she'd be able to sleep. Rachel rolled out of bed and walked downstairs. The kitchen was dark and she pulled open the refrigerator door and let the cool air rush out.

The pitcher of lemonade looked appealing and she set it on the counter, then pulled out a package of string cheese. She found a glass and a plate and added a few crackers, then carried the food out to the porch.

After living in the heart of Chicago, she was always amazed at how silent the world could be. It almost hurt her ears to search for a noise. A dog barked in the distance, the sound traveling in the still air.

"Can't sleep?"

The sound of his voice startled her. He sat on one of the wicker chairs at the end of the porch. He was wearing just his boxers, his bare feet resting on the porch rail, a bottle of beer in his hand.

"You scared me."

"Sorry. I came over to get something to drink. It's so hot I can't sleep."

The sky flashed. "Heat lightning. I don't think it's going to cool down."

She held out the plate to him as she sat down, and he took a piece of string cheese. "I have to get some of this to take home with me," he said.

"You can probably get it in Seattle," she said. "You just haven't looked for it."

He took a bite, then a sip of his beer. "You know

what I'd like to do? For the next seventeen days, I'd like to forget that I'm leaving. I'd like to pretend that the bus ticket I have back to Seattle doesn't exist. I'd like to just live each day without thinking about the next."

"That might be difficult to do," Rachel said.

"Why can't we do what feels right?" he said. "Why do we have to deny ourselves?"

Rachel's breath caught in her throat and she quickly drew another. Why? Was it really going to change anything? It wouldn't lessen the loneliness she'd feel after he left, so why bother to protect herself?

He was right. She could deal with the pain when it came. But until then, she'd revel in the passion that this man had brought into her life. "All right," she said. "But you have to promise me something."

"Anything," Dermot said.

"When it comes time to leave, you'll just go. You'll walk away and there won't be any long goodbyes or promises that we'll see each other again. You'll just disappear and not come back."

"Rachel, I—"

"Those are my terms," she said.

He considered her offer, then nodded. "All right. I can live with that."

Rachel set the snack down on the small table between the wicker chairs, then slowly stood. She walked to his chair and, straddling his legs, sat down on his lap. "I think I want you to kiss me now."

Dermot stared up at her, then reached to touch her breast. He cupped her warm flesh, running his thumb over her nipple until it became a stiff peak beneath the thin cotton of her nightgown. He smoothed his hand along her hip, his fingers soft and teasing.

Rachel could feel his hard shaft between them, straining against the front of his boxers. When he was with her, it never took much for Dermot to get aroused. Rachel had never had that power with a man before. There was a certain satisfaction in knowing that she could have Dermot whenever she wanted him, that he would be there, ready and willing to fulfill her every need. Dermot moaned softly as she reached between them and wrapped her fingers around his heat.

Already, his body was so familiar to her. She knew how he'd react to her touch, the way his breath would catch in his throat, the sound of his voice whispering her name.

"Three days has been too long," she murmured.

Dermot grabbed her waist and stood, wrapping her legs around his hips. He backed her up against the wall of the house and kissed the curve of her neck and then moved lower, teasing at her breast with his tongue. "Your bed or mine?" he asked as he gently caressed her nipple.

"Let's stay right here," she said. "It's too hot inside."

He groaned softly, his kiss growing more urgent, and he dragged his tongue along the crease of her mouth until she surrendered completely. Her knees went soft and she felt herself melt in his arms.

"Why did we ever stop doing this?" she murmured.

"I can't remember. But we won't make that mistake again, will we?"

"No," Rachel said.

He slowly trailed kisses over her shoulder and down her arm. Then, he set her back on her feet and knelt in front of her, pushing her nightgown up around her hips. Rachel raked her fingers through his hair, anticipating what he was about to do to her.

He was so beautiful, so incredibly sexy. She couldn't imagine ever feeling this attracted to a man again. There seemed to be electricity that crackled between them every time they were together. Just one touch of his fingers to her bare skin was all it took for the attraction to overwhelm them both.

"I need you," he murmured. "I need to fall asleep with you in my arms and wake up the same way."

Rachel understood how he felt. The luxury of spending an entire night together in bed was one they'd grown very fond of. "We have to get up early to do chores," she said. "Will you promise not to keep me up too late?"

He looked up at her. "Why? Would it be so bad if we spent the whole night making love?"

Dermot's kisses trailed lower, until he found the damp spot between her legs. She was already aroused, and the moment his tongue touched her there, her body jerked in response.

"I love that I can touch you like this," he said. "That there's nothing left to stop us." He gently parted her legs, tasting her until she writhed against the wall, her knees weak and her body burning.

"Oh," she breathed. "Oh, right there."

As he brought her closer and closer to her release, Rachel murmured his name urgently. Dermot followed her cues, dragging her back from the edge when she got too close. It wasn't enough. She didn't want to experience this pleasure by herself.

She reached out and tangled her fingers in his hair, tugging until he looked up at her. He knew what she wanted without her even needing to tell him, and he stood and drew her leg up along his hip.

"It's all right," she said. "You don't have to worry."

"Are you sure?"

Rachel nodded. She'd been on the pill for years and it had always seemed like such a practical thing. But now, it was liberating. She trusted Dermot and he trusted her. She wanted to experience him without any barriers between them. Rachel didn't care what came later as long as this came now.

She gently guided him to her entrance and Dermot closed his eyes the moment they touched. Slowly, exquisitely, he pushed inside of her. Rachel felt the muscles in his body tense, but he didn't give in. Instead, he slowly began to move.

She closed her eyes and focused on the sensations that washed over her body. She was already so close, but this seemed to take her to a higher level, the need growing more intense with each stroke. This was paradise, she thought. There was nothing more perfect.

"I want you," he murmured. "Come for me."

He increased his pace and Rachel felt herself dancing on the edge. And when release came, it came so fast that it caught her by surprise. She cried out and the pleasure shook her body, stealing her ability to think.

It was enough to send him over the edge and Dermot surrendered a moment later. It was simple, uncomplicated and pure, the two of them searching for release and finding it with each other.

He was craving what she could only satisfy for a short time. Though she felt sated now, Rachel knew that she'd want more. He untangled her leg from around his waist and nuzzled into the curve of her neck. "Can we stay here forever?" he asked.

"I think maybe we could," Rachel joked.

They stood there for a long time, his forehead pressed against hers, his hand braced beside her head. Rachel listened to his breathing. She wondered what he was thinking. But she was afraid to ask. Instead, she pressed a kiss into the center of his chest.

"You know what I could go for? A nice, cool bath."

He reached down and grabbed her hand. "Lead the way."

6

"ARE YOU GOING TO tell me where we're going?" Dermot asked as he slid behind the wheel of the pickup.

"We're going on a field trip," Rachel said.

They'd finished the milking for the morning and Rachel had ordered him out of his barn clothes and into something "decent." At first Dermot had assumed they were going into town for breakfast, but she'd fed him at the kitchen table, perching on a chair and staring at him until he finished.

"I always hated field trips in school. We never went anywhere interesting."

"What would you consider interesting?"

"The zoo? Maybe a natural history museum? Even a decent library."

"Then you're probably not going to like this." She pointed to the ignition. "Start the truck. We're heading west."

Dermot drove the pickup out of the driveway and

headed away from Mapleton. "So, what am I going to learn today? It's not a field trip unless I learn something."

She sighed in frustration. "You're going to learn to be patient and enjoy the ride."

He chuckled softly. "I already know how to do that. I do that every night with you."

"Funny," she said. "And this comes because all you think about is sex. This is about business. I have to go sign a new contract with Briar Hollow Cheese. We sell our milk to them. You'll get a chance to taste some of their cheese."

"Cool," he said. "I knew I'd get it out of you."

"They make chèvre, which is traditional goat cheese. And also feta and bouchon, which is like parmesan cheese. We'll bring some home and I'll make something with it tonight. And I want to send some home with you, too. So you have something to remember us by."

"I don't need cheese to remember you," he said. "I've got a lot of other things I'll remember."

"Like what?" she asked.

"Oh, let me see. I'll remember how your hair smells in the morning when I wake up and you've stolen my pillow. And I'll remember the sound of your laugh when you're watching the kids scamper around their pen. I'll remember sitting across from you in the evening and sharing supper together." He paused. "I'll even remember this."

Rachel slid over and sat next to him, dropping a kiss on his cheek. "Good. I'm happy to hear that."

The drive to the cheese factory was passed with lighthearted chatter. Now that they'd actually decided not to think about the future, it took some of the pressure off them both. Dermot was happy, but he could see that there were moments where Rachel wasn't so enthusiastic. Something he said or did would put her in a dark mood for a short time and he'd have to tease her out of it. He felt like he was rearranging the deck chairs on the Titanic.

Briar Hollow was a small operation, set close to the road in a rural area. Dermot pulled into the parking lot and then hopped out and circled around the truck. He opened the door for Rachel and grabbed her around the waist, setting her on the ground.

"You'll like Ben," she said. "He's a real artisan. Every year, he goes to France for a few weeks and studies cheese making with a master. His cheeses are used in a lot of the best restaurants in Chicago."

A bell above the door rang as they entered. Rachel introduced him to Ben's daughter, Ellen, who stood behind the counter. "This is my friend Dermot Quinn. He's been working at the farm, but he's leaving in a couple weeks. I wanted to send some cheese home to Seattle with him."

Ellen regarded him with a curious look, then held out her hand. "A pleasure to meet you, Dermot. You two just take whatever you want from the cases. I'll get you a box."

"Ben called me. I'm here to sign another contract," Rachel added.

Ellen handed her a box. "I'll tell Ben you're here."

They walked around the shop and Rachel fed Dermot little samples from glass-covered dishes. When Ben walked into the shop, she introduced the men and they all sat down together. "Dermot's learning a little more about the dairy," Rachel explained.

"Good," Ben said. "Well, there's something I wanted to talk to you about. Something very important."

"What is it?" Rachel asked, worried at the serious tone in his voice.

"We just took on a new wholesaler. They're going to give us a national brand so we need more from each of our dairies. Over the next year, we'd like to see you double your production." Rachel gasped and he held up his hand. "Now, I know your situation. But this would increase your profit margins, which might make it possible for you to hire the help you need."

Dermot looked at the stricken expression on Rachel's face. "I—I don't think I can do it, Ben," she said. "I'd love to help you out, but there just aren't enough hours in the day."

Dermot cleared his throat. "Wait a second. Rachel, we can figure out a—"

Rachel quickly stood. "Can I have some time to think about this?"

"Sure," Ben said. "Here's the contract. And you know we'll buy whatever milk Clover Meadow produces. You're one of our best dairies. We'll just be paying more to those dairies that produce more for us. Heck, my daughter, Ellen, and her husband are even thinking about getting into the dairy business. And we'll be adding to our operation. Another five thousand square feet."

"Great," Rachel said.

She quickly walked out to the parking lot, forgetting the box of cheese that they'd collected. When she reached the truck, her face was pale and she was gasping for breath. Dermot bent her over at the waist, lowering her head. "Breathe," he ordered.

"I—I can't. I've been trying to think of a way to milk fewer goats, not more. I can't do this. I never wanted to be a goat farmer. Why did my father do this to me?"

When she looked up, her eyes were full of tears. "My life is all laid out for me. I'm never going to get off the farm. I'm going to be milking goats for the rest of my life."

Dermot dragged her into his arms and held her tight. "I'm sure he never wanted you to be unhappy, sweetheart. You know that. Maybe he just wanted to make sure his animals would live out their lives on your farm."

She sniffled and looked up at him through watery eyes. "You think?"

"I think," Dermot reassured her. "If you can find someone to buy the farm who wants to keep the goats, then I think maybe your father would be happy. Remember what Ben said?" he continued. "Ellen and her husband have been looking around for a farm of their own. They want to start a goat dairy. Why don't you let them know that you might consider selling?"

She thought about his suggestion. "My brothers and sister would certainly be happy. And I know Ellen and Kyle. I've met their two children. They're definitely goat people." She paused. "We'd have to make arrangements for Eddie. He's not going to want to leave the farm. He's lived there his entire life."

"I'm sure you could work something out," he said. "Now, we forgot our cheese inside. I think we should go back and talk to Ellen about your farm. You don't have to decide right now, but you could let her know it might be an option."

"I really haven't thought seriously about selling," she said. "I made a promise to myself that I'd stay at least a year before I made any decisions."

"And how long have you been running the farm?" he asked.

"Almost a year?"

"There you go." He tipped her face up and wiped the tears away with his fingertips. "Come on, let's go back inside and see what she has to say."

But now that the idea had found a place in her mind, Dermot began to question his reasons for suggesting it. Was he really interested in her happiness or were his motives purely selfish? If she didn't have the farm, then she was free to move wherever she wanted—to Seattle, perhaps?

He wasn't going to deny that he'd spent some time imagining what life would be like living in his house instead of hers. As much as he loved the farm and the animals, he was starting to realize how much his grandfather's business meant to him. Maybe it was in his genes. The Quinn family had been on the water for generations, first as fishermen in Bantry Bay and now as boat builders. Like Rachel, he had family traditions to uphold.

Dermot opened the door for Rachel. When they got back inside, he pressed his hand to the small of her back, hoping to calm her emotions with his touch.

"You're back!" Ellen said. "You forgot your cheese."

"I know," Rachel said. "I wanted to talk to you before I left. Ben mentioned that you and Kyle might be looking for a farm, a place to raise goats."

Ellen nodded. "We've been looking. It's been difficult. We've seen a few places but they haven't been… perfect. It's a huge risk and an even bigger investment. My father has agreed to help, but we plan to spend the rest of our lives on the place, so it has to be just right." She laughed. "Like Clover Meadow."

"Well, I'm glad to hear that. Because I've been thinking about selling."

Ellen gasped, her eyes opening wide. "Oh, my gosh. Really?"

Rachel nodded. "I'm still weighing all my options, but…well, don't buy a place until you've talked to me first. Could you do that?"

"Yes, yes. Of course."

"And don't tell Ben. Let's keep this between us. You, me and Kyle?"

"Sure. I know how the gossip gets around. I promise to keep this strictly confidential."

"Good," Rachel said. She grabbed the box. "Thank you, Ellen. And I guess we'll be talking in the future."

Ellen smiled. "I sure hope so."

When they got outside, Dermot slipped his arm around her shoulders and pulled her close. "Are you all right?"

Rachel nodded. "I feel…relieved. Like a weight has been lifted. I suddenly have options."

"Options," he said.

"I think we should go out for lunch. My treat. There's a great drive-in in Elkhorn. They have the best cheese curds," she added.

"I am beginning to love cheese," Dermot teased, grabbing the box from her arms. "Bring it on."

Rachel leaned in and stole a kiss. "Come on, then. I'm hungry."

As they drove down the country road, Dermot

turned up the radio and sang along with a love song. The windows were open and the warm breeze buffeted through the truck. It was another perfect day, he thought to himself. There wouldn't be many of them left. But now he had even more reason to hope that he might not have to count the days. Rachel might be his forever.

THE FEDEX TRUCK RUMBLED into the yard at exactly 10:00 a.m. Dermot and Rachel were walking back from the barn, Benny trailing after them. Rachel shaded her eyes against the morning sun. "I wonder what this is about."

No doubt another missive from her siblings' lawyers. The last time they'd sent registered mail. Now they were assaulting her with overnight packages. She thought they might finally give up now that Jane wanted to send her two sons to live at Clover Meadow. The balance of power had definitely shifted.

The driver hopped out of the truck and circled around to meet her in the middle of the drive. "Rachel Howe?" he asked.

"That's me," she said. She signed for the envelope, then took it from his hands. But it wasn't from a lawyer. "This is odd," she said to Dermot, staring at the bill of lading.

"What is it?" he asked.

"It's from some kind of literary agency. Lynn Barrett Literary Agency in New York. Have you written a book that I don't know about?"

"No. I never kiss and tell. What about you?"

She shook her head. "I wouldn't have the words to describe it all."

"Hmm. Maybe you should give it a try. Talk dirty to me and all kinds of interesting things might happen." He growled softly, then pulled her into his arms.

Rachel slipped out of his grasp. "You are going to have to learn to behave yourself, Mr. Quinn. If Jane is sending her boys here, we can't have them corrupted by your out-of-control libido."

"I'll have you know, my libido was well under control until I met you."

Rachel opened the envelope and reached inside to pull out a smaller one. Inside was a letter and she skimmed it as they walked to the porch. "Oh, my God," she said, sitting down on the step. "They want to know if I'd be interested in illustrating a children's book." Rachel reread the letter. "Remember I told you about that publisher I talked to at the convention? She passed my card on to one of her authors. She's asking if I have an agent." She looked up at Dermot. "I can't believe all of this is happening now."

"This is a good thing. Do you have an agent?"

"No. I work with the greeting card publisher direct. Now Briar Hollow wants me to buy more goats. And then, in between milking goats and drawing skunks and ducks, and caring for two high school–age boys,

I'm supposed to illustrate a children's book." She groaned. "Maybe in my spare time I could go to medical school and rewire the house."

Dermot laughed, pulling her close. "It always helps to overreact, Rachel. Just throw all your insecurities out there and see what sticks."

"I'm not overreacting," she protested. "Don't you see what's happening? I'm going to have to make a choice. The farm or my art. One or the other. I can't continue to do both. And this is a really good opportunity."

"You'll figure out a way."

"How?"

"I'll stay a little longer than I originally planned."

"No," Rachel said. "No, that is not a solution. You have your own life to get back to and I'm not going—"

"But I kind of like living here in the middle of your life," he said. "Mostly, I like sleeping in the middle of your bed."

Rachel had already decided that she wasn't going to take advantage of him any longer. He was far too kind to her, and though it made life easier, she had to figure out these things on her own.

"I'm going to turn it down," she said.

"You don't even know what it's about," Dermot reminded. "Why don't you find out before you make a decision that you might regret?"

She met his gaze. He was right, of course. Dermot was always right. He took a measured approach to any decision, weighing all his options, examining the pros and cons. Rachel suspected if he were the one running the farm, they'd be milking two hundred goats, turning out cases of soap and making their own cheese. "All right. I won't make any quick decisions. But all of this is making me a little nervous."

"We'll go into town later and post another ad at the grocery store. And then, we'll put an ad in the local papers. And we'll find someone to help you out on the farm."

Rachel leaned over a dropped a kiss on his lips. "You're really too good to me, you know that, don't you?"

"I have ulterior motives," he said, a wicked smile curling the corners of his mouth. "Which I am about to reveal."

"You smell like a goat," she said. "I smell like a goat."

"We could always take a shower," he suggested. "Together."

Right now, she didn't want to think about all the things she had to do, all the decisions she had to make. She just wanted to lose herself in an intriguing exploration of Dermot's incredible body. Rachel tugged off her boots and set them on the steps. "I'll race you."

She ran inside, pulling her T-shirt over her head as she hurried through the kitchen. Dermot followed, hot on her heels, nearly catching her on the stairs. She screamed as she eluded his grasp, then slipped into the bathroom and shut the door behind her.

"There's only enough hot water for me," she called. "You'll have to wait."

"Come on, Rachel. We can share a shower, can't we?"

"You know what happened the last time we did that. We got distracted and ran out of hot water before I even got my hair washed."

"I promise. I'll keep my hands to myself this time around."

"Promise?"

"I'm taking my clothes off right now," he said. "I'm almost naked. Oh, yes, now I'm naked."

She opened the bathroom door a crack and peeked out. He was standing in the hallway, his clothes at his feet. "Can I come in?"

Her fingers twitched with the urge to touch him. He was already aroused. With Dermot, it was easy, she mused. He made it obvious that he wanted her as much as she wanted him. When it came to sex, she didn't have to think. She just felt.

She opened the door wider to let him pass. As he did, Rachel let her hand drift across his belly. He moaned and turned into her touch.

"I'm counting on you to behave," she said in her most seductive tone.

"Then stop messing with me," he replied. Dermot reached behind the shower curtain and turned on the water.

Rachel quickly skimmed her jeans to the floor, then kicked them aside along with her socks. "I'm just making sure you're only interested in a shower."

Dermot grabbed her and kissed her, stopping her come-on with his lips and his tongue. When he finally drew away, Rachel stepped behind the curtain and into the claw-foot tub. He joined her a moment later, wrapping his arms around her waist. His mouth found hers again and he kissed her, hungry with desire. Rachel arched against him as his lips trailed over her shoulder and onto her breasts.

She slowly stroked him as he explored her body with his lips and tongue. The water made him slick, and before long, he was fully aroused and moaning with desire. Rachel knew exactly what would drive him wild, and when she closed her lips over the head of his shaft, he gasped, his hands braced on her shoulders, his eyes closed.

If this was the last man she'd know intimately, Rachel could live with that. The memories of what they shared were so deeply etched into her mind that she knew she'd be able to recall every caress, every reaction, by just closing her eyes.

She tempted him with her lips and her tongue, surprised by how easily she could bring him to the edge. And then, she took him too close. Dermot grabbed her arms and pulled her to her feet, his eyes closed, his jaw tense. Rachel watched as he struggled to maintain control.

He gently drew her against his body, her back to him, his fingers slipping between her legs. Every nerve in her body tingled, his touch causing her pulse to race. He could read her reactions, and when she had reached the point of no return, Dermot slipped inside her.

The feel of him buried deep was almost more than she could take. The fears and insecurities that had kept her from loving him were gone. Why couldn't she feel like this all the time, as if there were no way anything could come between them?

The sensations coursing through her body obliterated rational thought, and a moment later, she was caught in the vortex of her release. Rachel's body went boneless and it was all she could do to stay upright. A moment later, he found his own release, his hands clutching her hips as he drove into her one last time.

They clung to each other beneath the shower, her backside nestled in his lap, both of them trembling in the aftermath of their orgasms. It would never be like this with another man, she mused. The passion they shared was singular and powerful, and becoming more frightening to her with every encounter they shared. How would she ever do without this?

Though she wanted to imagine a happy ending for the two of them, the odds didn't seem to favor them.

Was she willing to give up everything she'd known, everything she promised, to find a life with him? And was he ready to make that kind of commitment?

There were too many questions left unanswered and she was running out of time to ask them all.

THE STORM BEGAN IN the middle of the night. Lightning flashed and the thunder was so loud it rattled the windows. Dermot sat up in bed, reaching out for Rachel. But her side of the bed was empty.

He tossed the sheet aside and stood, searching the room for something to wear. In the end, he pulled on a pair of jeans and walked downstairs barefoot. He found her, curled up in front of the television, tuned to the weather channel. "What's going on?" he asked.

"Tornado warning," she said.

"Tornado? Really? How close?"

She pointed to the television. "About twenty miles." Rachel drew her knees up, wrapping her arms around her legs. "I hate bad weather," she said. "In town, they have the sirens to warn you. But out here, you just have to listen to the storm. It was so hot and humid today. I knew this was coming."

He sat down next to her, his gaze fixed on the television. "Are there a lot of tornadoes around here?"

Rachel nodded. "Sure. We get some each summer. They don't always do a lot of damage." She shuddered. "I was terrified of tornadoes when I was younger. My dad would listen to the radio and wake us up in the middle of the night and we'd go down into the cellar and wait for the storm to pass. My mother would sing songs and try to distract me, but it didn't help."

"We don't really have tornadoes in Seattle," he said.

"Spring is usually the worst," she said. "But a few years ago, we had a tornado in October. It tore the roof off a barn not far from here." She snuggled up against him. "I think I watched *The Wizard of Oz* too many times when I was a kid. Between the tornado and the flying monkeys, I couldn't sleep for days."

Dermot wrapped his arms around her. "You don't have to be scared," he said. "I'll protect you."

"You can't protect me from tornadoes." She sighed softly. "What about you? Aren't you afraid of anything?"

"Nothing. I'm made of steel," he teased. "They call me Superman back in Seattle."

Rachel wove her fingers through his. "Tell me."

Dermot hesitated for a long moment. They'd been so intimate, and yet neither one of them had confessed their deepest fears. They'd both carefully avoided revealing too much. Maybe it was time. "I'm… I'm afraid that if I love something too much, I'll lose it."

"So you never fall in love?" she asked.

He shook his head. "I try very hard not to."

"Interesting," she said.

"That's your reply? 'Interesting'?"

She snuggled closer. "It doesn't surprise me, considering what happened with your parents. Especially at such a young age. I'm surprised you're as normal as you are."

"What about you?"

"I think loss is something farm kids deal with at an \ age. We see the circle of life all the time. Animals that we love die. We cry and then move on. That doesn't mean it becomes any easier, but it's... understood?"

"What scares you, Rachel? Besides tornadoes?" He waited for her answer, wondering what she'd say. Dermot had never met a woman as strong as Rachel Howe, as stubborn or determined.

"I'm afraid that I'll be alone. I'll be like Eddie, regretting all the mistakes I made in life, wondering how things might have been different." She drew a ragged breath. "I'm happy, don't get me wrong. But I'm afraid that, someday, I'll wake up and it will be too late."

"That will never happen," Dermot said. He wanted to say more, to tell her how much she meant to him, to make her understand that if he could ever love anyone it would be her.

Dermot could imagine a future with her, a life that included more happiness than he'd ever had in the past. He had never had a serious relationship. There'd been dating relationships, and sexual relationships, but none of them ventured into the realm of "emotional."

Yet, when he was with Rachel, he didn't want to be anywhere else. If he were honest, he was almost afraid to leave her, afraid that what they had found together might suddenly evaporate. At this point in every other relationship, he was usually looking for a way out. But with Rachel, he was still trying to figure a way in.

Neither one of them had any expectations, beyond hard work and constant companionship. And when there was a promise of more, he accepted their relationship for what it was—for as long as it lasted.

Was that why he was so confused? Without a point of reference, he had no way of judging what they shared together. Was this love? Friendship? Or just sexual desire being satisfied? Suddenly, it was important to put a name to it.

A clap of thunder shook the house and Rachel jumped, groaning softly. Dermot took her hand in his. "Come on."

"No, I'm not going to bed until this is over."

"This will help. I promise."

Reluctantly, she followed him into the kitchen. He opened the door and rain-damp wind buffeted them both. The sky was a riot of light, each flash illuminating the huge clouds. The air was full of electricity.

"I'm not going out there," she said.

"We're just going to stand on the porch. If it gets

really bad, we'll come back in. I promise. Trust me, Rachel."

He held out his hand and she reluctantly stepped outside. Dermot wrapped his arms around her waist. "Now, we just have to wait for the next big flash of lightning and—" The sky split open and he yanked her into a long, deep kiss. He continued through the thunder crack, distracting her with his lips and his tongue.

When it was over, Dermot stepped back. "Wait for it."

"What are you doing?"

"You'll see. You'll never—" The lightning flashed and he kissed her again, the thunder calling an end to the kiss. "From now on, whenever you're in the middle of a storm, you'll think of kissing me. You won't be able to help yourself."

"You're crazy," she said.

Another bolt of lightning flashed in the sky and she barely noticed. "See," Dermot said, "it's working."

She turned and walked along the porch railing, staring out into the storm as if the answers were all there. "It is beautiful," she finally said, the wind whipping at her hair. "Powerful. Exciting." She paused. "And dangerous. Kind of like you."

"I'm not dangerous, Rachel."

"You are," she insisted. "You have no idea. You

make me need you. The more time I spend with you, the more I can't do without you."

"That's usually the way it is," Dermot said. "What's wrong with that?"

"Because I feel completely safe with you, too. I don't understand how that can be. I don't know why I feel this way. I'll never be able to forget you."

"Then don't. Don't forget a single moment."

The wind shifted suddenly and Rachel glanced over at him. "It's coming now. You can smell it."

In a matter of seconds the storm had whipped itself into a fury. The rain was driven sideways and the maples around the house rocked and bent to the breaking point. A limb snapped and fell near the end of the porch and debris blew across the yard. In the distance, he heard the goats bleating from the barn.

"We better get back inside," he said.

Rachel shook her head. "No. I want to face this fear. You were right."

"I might have been wrong." Dermot grabbed her hand and dragged her to the door, pushing her back into the kitchen. He peered out the window, stunned to see that the wind was blowing even harder. "Maybe we should go in the cellar."

He opened the door and flipped on the light and followed Rachel to the bottom of the steps. They sat down on the last one. A few seconds later, the stairwell went dark.

"There's a flashlight at the top of the stairs," she said. "I'll get it."

"No, stay here," he said, holding tight to her hand.

"Are you afraid?"

"Yeah, I'm kind of creeped out. I saw that movie *Twister*. I'm just waiting for the house to disintegrate around us. Are the goats going to be all right?"

"Yes," she said, her voice coming out of the dark. "They'll go in the barn. The stone foundation is strong. They'll huddle up in a corner."

He wrapped his arms around her and pulled her close, the two of them listening to the storm raging outside. And when it was over, they climbed the stairs and walked outside to survey the damage from the porch.

Small branches and clumps of maple leaves were scattered over the yard but all the buildings were still standing, their roofs intact. The cushions from the wicker chairs on the porch had disappeared and one of the hanging pots had fallen into the garden, but that was the limit of the damage.

He turned her to face him and kissed her softly. "That was kind of scary," he admitted.

"I told you. Flying monkeys all over again." She drew a deep breath of the cool air. "Smell the ozone? It's from the lightning."

Dermot slipped his arm around her shoulders and they walked back inside. A breeze now drifted through the screen door, taking the humidity out of the air. The storm was a reflection of their relationship, he mused. All the wild, crazy emotions one minute and the beautiful calm the next.

And yet, there was a danger there. He couldn't predict the weather and he didn't know exactly what was lurking just beyond the horizon—fair weather or the storm of the century?

7

THE TWO TEENAGE BOYS stood in the yard, staring at their mother's car as it pulled out onto the road and drove off. Rachel held her breath, trying to think of something to say that might erase the fearful expressions from their faces.

She hadn't seen her nephews in six or seven years and she barely recognized them. Trevor, the eldest, was nearly sixteen, and as tall as Dermot, well over six feet. Taylor was a year younger and appeared to be the more sensitive of the pair, tears swimming in his eyes as he tried to be brave.

Rachel glanced over at Dermot. He'd been a teenage boy at one time. Maybe he knew what to say. The last thing she wanted to do was cause them more emotional upset. She drew a deep breath and pasted a smile on her face. "Why don't I show you your room. You can get settled and then I'll make you something to eat. Are you hungry?"

Trevor shook his head. "No. We ate lunch on the road."

"I—I'm kinda hungry," Taylor said.

"No," Trevor whispered. "We're not hungry. It's all right. We can wait until dinner."

"Come on, then," she said.

Trevor picked up the single suitcase they'd brought along and then hitched his backpack onto his other shoulder. Taylor had a backpack of his own.

"I'm going to check the goats," Dermot said. "We could really use your help in the barn, guys. If you're up for it, why don't you change and come out after you've had something to eat."

"Okay," Trevor said. He put his arm around Taylor's shoulders as they climbed the porch steps.

Rachel held the screen door open for them. When they reached the top of the stairs, she pointed to the room across the hall from her bedroom. "I hope you don't mind sharing. It's the only room with two beds."

Trevor stood in the doorway, taking in the surroundings. "It's good," he said.

"Good," Taylor repeated. "Do you have Wi-Fi?"

"Wi-Fi? No," Rachel said. "There's a cable hookup in the kitchen. That's usually where I work. You're welcome to use my computer to write to your friends or go online."

"We brought our own laptops," Taylor said. "I can hook up Wi-Fi if you want. I brought along my router and modem if you have broadband."

"All right," Rachel said with a smile. "That would be really nice. You sound like you know what you're doing with computers."

Taylor returned her smile. "I'm pretty good at computers. I built my own CPU. I couldn't bring it along, though."

"So are you going to do your school work on your computer?" Rachel asked.

"We stopped at the school and mom enrolled us," Trevor said. "Didn't she tell you?"

Rachel shook her head. Jane had been so distraught that she'd barely said a word. She was doing all she could to keep from breaking down and Rachel could do nothing but reassure her that she'd take good care of the boys. "That's good. It's Friday. We could go to the football game tonight. Maybe you'd have a chance to meet some of the kids?" Trevor gave Taylor an uneasy look and Rachel quickly shook her head. "Maybe it's best to just get to know the farm first. Why don't you unpack and then come down when you're ready?"

She walked out of the bedroom and hurried down the stairs. Dermot was pacing the porch as she stepped outside. "I have no idea what I'm doing. They seem so fragile and terrified. I don't know what to say."

"Just leave them alone for now," he said. "Let them lean on each other. Their whole world has been turned upside down. They don't know who to trust."

Rachel grabbed his hand and held it to her heart. "I'm so glad you're here."

Dermot pulled her toward him and kissed her forehead. "Why don't you make them something to eat.
Even though they say they're not hungry, boys that
age will always eat if you put something in front of
them. I'm going to go work on replacing that window
in the milk house that got broken in the storm." He
kissed her again, this time on the mouth, his tongue
teasing at hers. "What are we going to do about this?"
he murmured.

"I'll meet you right here, after they've gone to bed.
I'll bring the wine. You bring yourself."

"It's a date."

He walked down the steps and Rachel smiled to
herself. There had been so much going on at the farm
lately that she'd forgotten he'd be leaving in another
week. If she had the power to stop time, she'd turn
off all the clocks at this very moment.

She was happy and hopeful and only a bit worried about the decisions she'd have to make about
her future. And she was falling in love with Dermot
Quinn. Rachel giggled, then spun around and went
in to gather things to make sandwiches. It was appar-
ent that Dermot was just as smitten as she was. And
she had to believe that once he left, he'd realize the
depth of his feeling for her.

"Absence makes the heart grow fonder," she reminded herself.

Rachel was counting on that. Their relationship
was like dream, a fantasy come true. And though they

both lived in the real world, the passion they shared was something very special. Would a life with Dermot ever be "normal"? Would their desire for each other fade over time?

A shiver prickled her skin. Just the thought of him touching her caused an instant reaction. Rachel arranged sliced ham on whole-wheat bread. She'd have to ask if the boys liked mayo or mustard. "Potato chips." She grabbed a bag that Dermot had brought home from the grocery store, then set the cookie jar on the table and peeked inside to see that it was well stocked with the chocolate chip cookies she'd made a few days before.

Rachel walked to the stairs, but stopped herself from calling to Trevor and Taylor. She'd follow Dermot's advice when it came to the boys. He'd been exactly where they were years ago. He knew what they were going through.

She grabbed her sketchbook and sat down at the kitchen table, then turned to the illustration she'd been working on. Beavers. Rachel smiled. With their funny teeth and flat tails, they made for a humorous image, one that would find its way onto a greeting card sometime next year.

"What are you drawing?"

Rachel glanced up to find Trevor standing in the doorway of the kitchen. She held out the sketchbook. "Beavers," she said. "I mostly draw animals. I've been working on squirrels, too."

"Wow," he murmured. "These are good."

"Do you like to draw?"

He nodded. "I mostly draw robots and alien creatures."

"I'd like to see your drawings," she said.

He shrugged. "I left them at home."

Rachel pushed back from the table and crossed to the desk at the far end of the kitchen. She grabbed a fresh sketchbook and her box of colored pencils, then returned to the table. "Here," she said. "Take these."

"Really?"

Rachel nodded. "Yes. You should pursue your drawing while you're here. When I was younger, I used to draw all the time. You never know where it will lead. When I got out of high school, I went to art school in Chicago. And now I draw greeting cards." She shrugged. "Well, why don't you have something to eat. It will be a while until dinner. We have to do the milking first. Where is Taylor?"

"He fell asleep. He was really upset in the car. All the crying kinda wore him out."

"It's good that he has you," Rachel said.

Trevor nodded, then sat down at the table and grabbed a sandwich. He gobbled it down in huge bites and Rachel quickly poured him a glass of milk. He ate a second sandwich, then polished off a handful of potato chips and four cookies, before he was sated.

"Feeling better?" she asked.

He nodded. "I'm gonna go out and see the goats."

Rachel wanted to tell him to change his clothes, but then decided against it. "There are some rubber boots in the milk house. Take off your shoes and find a pair that fits before you walk through the barn. You don't want to step in goat poop your first day on the farm."

Trevor headed out the door and Rachel cleaned up the mess from his lunch. Then she put a plate together, poured another glass of milk and took it upstairs to Taylor. As Trevor had said, he was sprawled across the bed, sound asleep. She set the meal on the bedside table, then pulled the shades against the afternoon sun.

As she watched him sleep, she thought about Dermot and everything he'd gone through as a kid. It was difficult enough losing her parents and they'd lived a long and happy life. But Dermot's parents had just sailed away, never to return, leaving four young boys to grieve their loss.

Tears pressed at the corners of her eyes and she swallowed the lump of emotion in her throat. Until Jane returned, she'd do her best for Trevor and Taylor. She'd try to be a friend and a confidante, and someone they could trust with their feelings.

She walked to the bedroom door and took one last look at her nephew. He was family. And though she'd once thought she'd lost most of her family, she realized that wasn't true. She had two nephews and a sister who needed her. And she intended to do everything she could to make their lives happier.

DERMOT STOOD BACK and watched as Trevor guided a goat into the milking stanchion. "There you go," he said. "You've got it now. Show her who's the boss."

Trevor locked the goat into the stanchion, then stepped away, a smile on his face. The goat bleated, the sound startling the boy. He jumped back, then turned to Dermot. "Did I hurt her?"

"Nope. She knows what she's supposed to do. But goats can be stubborn and willful. They're very clever, too. I was standing next to one of the goats a few days ago, and before I knew it, he'd eaten a hole in my shirt."

"Don't they eat everything?" Trevor asked.

"Pretty much. You have to be careful to keep the extra feed out of their way. They'll overeat and then they get bloat, which can be pretty serious. They'll find a way to crawl over a tall fence if they think it means more food. We lock everything up. That's very important."

As he explained some of the rules to Trevor, Dermot realized how much he'd learned about goat farming in a very short time. Rachel could leave Clover Meadow in his hands and he'd be able to run it on his own. He smiled to himself. Maybe he could treat Rachel to a day off before he left for good.

"How's it going?"

Rachel and Taylor walked in the door of the milking parlor, dressed in their rubber work boots. She walked over to Trevor and pointed to his brand-new

John Deere hat. "I see Eddie has given you the proper uniform."

Trevor nodded, then grabbed another hat from a nearby shelf. "Here, Taylor, this one's for you."

The younger boy put on the cap, then stood waiting for instructions. "Go ahead," Dermot said. "You show him what you learned. You know what you're doing."

Dermot moved to Rachel's side and watched as the boys brought the next ten goats into the milking parlor and locked them into the stanchions. Eddie then guided them through the steps on how to attach the milking machines, and by the time they got to the last goat, the first one was ready to move out the opposite door.

The two boys fell into a good pace and Eddie glanced over at Dermot and gave him a wink. "They learn a lot faster than you," he said with a grin.

"They had a better teacher," Dermot shot back.

"It looks like you've been made redundant."

Trevor glanced between the two of them, a worried expression on his face.

Dermot chuckled then pulled the brim of Trevor's cap over his eyes. "Hey, I'm happy to pass my responsibilities on to these two. I can spend more time putting those new downspouts on the old homestead." He grabbed Rachel's hand and pulled her along behind him, out of the barn and into the evening sunshine.

"Shouldn't we keep an eye on them?"

"Eddie's watching them. They'll be fine. They certainly don't need all three of us hovering over them."

"So, I guess we have some free time," Rachel said. "What are we going to do with ourselves?"

He draped his arm around her shoulders. "Let's take a walk."

"Where?"

"I don't know. Let's just see where we end up."

She slipped her arm around him and they walked past the barnyard and then turned north, toward her favorite spot on the creek.

"I think they're doing all right," Rachel said. "What do you think?"

"I think you're worrying far too much."

"This is a lot of responsibility," Rachel explained. "I'm the adult in charge. What if something goes wrong? What if they…do something bad?"

"Just what would you consider bad?" Dermot asked. "I'm very interested to hear this."

"I don't know. What if they get an F at school? Or they get in a fight? Or they swear at a teacher? There are a million things that could go wrong. God, being a parent must be sheer hell. No wonder my sister looked like such a wreck."

"It can't be that bad," Dermot said. "Most people seem to come through it without major problems."

"I don't know. Maybe I'm not cut out to be a mother. There's just too much that could go wrong. I'd be a bundle of nerves."

He dragged her into his arms and gave her a hug. "Rachel, you would be a fabulous mother."

"How do you know?"

"Because you're kind and compassionate and loving. A child would be lucky to have you for a mother."

She pushed up on her toes and gave him a quick kiss. "Have you ever thought about having children?"

"No, not really. Not until this afternoon. I was talking to Trevor and I was thinking, maybe I could do this. I think I'd have a lot to teach a kid."

"I guess it wouldn't be that much different than goats," Rachel said.

Dermot couldn't help but laugh. "Really?"

"You know what I mean. Goats can be very mischievous. And they never listen to what you say. And when they get sick they can't tell you what's wrong with them, you're just left guessing. And you spend a lot of time cleaning up after them."

"Goats are exactly like children," Dermot teased. "And husbands are exactly like donkeys and wives are exactly like chickens."

"You have that right," Rachel said with a nod. She set off across the field.

Dermot caught up to her and grabbed her hand. "So that's your opinion of marriage?"

"I have no opinion of marriage," Rachel said. "I think it can be harmful to develop an opinion of marriage before you've actually had a proposal. If that ever happens, then I figure I'll decide what I think."

She gave him a sideways glance. "Do you have an opinion you'd like to share?"

Dermot frowned. Considering her opinion, or non-opinion, maybe it was best that he kept his to himself. "No," he said. "I haven't thought much about it."

"It's a big risk," she said. "A leap of faith. I mean, my parents were married for forty-five years. How did they know that they weren't going to get bored with each other after ten or fifteen years. I buy a sofa that I love one day, and two months later, I think it's the ugliest sofa on the planet."

"Now men are no longer donkeys, they're sofas?"

"I'm just throwing out some analogies," she said.

"You're lucky you're such a good artist, because you suck at analogies," Dermot said.

Rachel giggled. "All right. Maybe I do. But the thought of mating for life is kind of scary. It's a long, long time."

"Penguins mate for life," he said. "I saw that on Nat. Geo."

"Eagles do, too. And geese. And swans."

They walked the rest of the way in silence, Dermot considering her comments. He'd never met someone he could imagine marrying, until now. In truth, he'd spent more time with Rachel than he had with any other woman in his life. Every day for almost six weeks. Almost every night, too. They were as close to married as he'd ever been and he hadn't thought once about running.

He raked his hand through his hair, stunned by the realization. In the past, he rarely continued a relationship after a few months. He grew bored and she grew clingy or they both were too busy to pursue anything further. But with Rachel, he'd stepped into her life one day and hadn't thought about leaving.

Five weeks together and he still looked forward to waking up with her beside him in the morning and falling asleep wrapped in her arms at night.

They reached the creek and Rachel sat down on a grassy spot near the bank. It was the kind of perfect scene that he would remember for a lifetime, the sun gleaming off the wet rocks, milkweed seeds floating on the air, and a sky so blue it hurt to look at it. And then there was Rachel, her pale hair caught up in a haphazard knot and her face flushed from the heat.

Dermot wandered to the edge of the water and picked up a wildflower from a clump on the creek bank. He'd grown so comfortable here on the farm and he tried to imagine Rachel in his environment. Could she ever feel the same way about Seattle?

As much as he tried, he couldn't seem to make the image jell in his mind. This was exactly where she belonged, in this place, on this farm. Dermot turned and looked at her, her gaze fixed somewhere on the horizon.

He'd never expected these choices to be easy. But then, he'd never expected them to be excruciatingly painful either. Once he fell in love, he'd just assumed it would all work out exactly as he wanted. He had a week left on the farm before he'd head home. She'd stay here forever, as she was always meant to.

There was only one thing he knew for certain. He'd have to learn to deal with the loss or spend the rest of his life wondering what might have been.

THE TOWN OF LAKE GENEVA was the closest thing to a tourist trap that could be found in the county. Known for its quaint shops, pretty streets and gleaming lake, Rachel usually made the short drive every few months to treat herself to a haircut or manicure.

Today she had Dermot, Trevor and Taylor for company. They'd stopped first at a discount store and picked up the list of school supplies she'd downloaded from the high school website, reassuring the boys that they would be ready when Monday rolled around.

After that, they'd enjoyed a leisurely lunch at a local hamburger joint, the boys inhaling their meal between one-word answers to Dermot's and Rachel's questions. Though they were feeling more comfortable at the farm, taking them out of that environment made her nephews a bit uneasy. And any discussion of school sent them both into a silent funk.

"Hey, there's a movie theater a few blocks from here," Rachel said. "Why don't we check what's on and if you guys want to see a movie, Dermot and I will do some more shopping."

"Yeah," Trevor said with a wide smile.

"What if I want to see the movie instead of going shopping with you?" Dermot asked.

That caused a laugh from Taylor. "Uh-oh," he murmured.

"I—I guess that would be all right," Rachel said. "I just thought you'd want to—" She forced a smile. "Never mind. I can shop on my own. I do it all the time."

Dermot grinned as he reached out and grabbed her hand. "I'm just teasing. Of course I'd love to go shopping with you, Aunt Rachel. It's my favorite thing to do in the whole world." Dermot rolled his eyes dramatically and Rachel threw a crumpled napkin at his face.

This caused the boys to dissolve into laughter, Dermot egging them on with silly faces. At heart, they were all just little boys, so easily amused. "Maybe I don't want you to come now," Rachel said.

"Aww," they all groaned in unison.

"I'm not sure I like this. Three against one." She stood up and grabbed the check. "Come on, let's get out of here. We don't want to be late for the movies."

In the end, the two boys decided to see the latest sci-fi action hit while Dermot was happy to accompany Rachel. They headed for her favorite antiques store, a small shop just off Main Street with wide plate-glass windows and an old-fashioned center entrance.

Dermot held open the door and ushered her inside.

Rachel walked right to the counter. Sylvia, the elderly woman who owned the store, was working behind the register. "Rachel. I didn't expect you to come in so soon. I just called on Friday."

"I was in town. And I wanted to see what you had."

"Come in back and I'll put it out over a table. It's really quite beautiful. One of the nicest I've seen."

Rachel had been buying antique quilts from Sylvia for almost a year, her only indulgence in a very strict budget. But her passion for collecting quilts had come from her mother. As a child, Rachel had accompanied her mother to auctions at least once a month in search of the hand-stitched creations.

Her first quilts had come from her grandmother, beautiful hand-pieced bedspreads made of faded calico fabrics. Then she'd inherited her mother's eclectic collection. And now she was adding quilts of her own.

Sylvia pulled the quilt from a bag and threw it over an antique dining table. She patted Rachel's shoulder. "I'll give you some time to enjoy it."

Rachel sighed. "Thank you, Sylvia."

Dermot stood by her side. "It's a quilt."

"It's a piece of American folk art," she said, smoothing her hands over the fabric. "It tells a story. All of these fabrics came from old clothing the family had worn. I use pencils and ink and they used old aprons and shirts and dresses. And the pattern represents the maker. And each region of the country has favorite patterns. The women worked together on the quilting. See these tiny little hand stitches? And the designs they make? It's beautiful." She stepped back and pointed to the price tag. "Tell me how much it is. I'm afraid to look."

Dermot glanced at the tag. "Four hundred," he said.

"I never pay more than three hundred." She shook her head. "I can't afford this one."

"But you want it."

"I can't have everything I want," Rachel said. "I have the farm and now the boys. There are just better ways to spend my money." Rachel shrugged. "Another one will come along."

"But you love this one," he said. "You should have this one."

His determination startled her. It was just a quilt. She'd passed on many of them before because of price or condition or budget considerations. She'd learned not to grow attached. "Another will come along. And it will be better than this."

With a soft curse, Dermot gathered the quilt up and tucked it under his arm. He carried it to the register and set it down, Rachel following hard on his heels. "What are you doing?"

"I'd like to buy this," he said. Dermot pulled his wallet out of his back pocket and laid down four hundred-dollar bills.

Rachel recognized the money immediately. It was

nearly all the money he'd made working on the farm. "What are you doing?"

"I'm buying you the quilt. You said you wanted it."

"I didn't want you to buy it for me," she said. "If I wanted it, I'd buy it myself." She put her hand over the quilt. "Sylvia, we're just going to talk about this for a bit, if you don't mind."

"Sylvia, I've made up my mind," Dermot countered. "I want the quilt. Please put it in a nice bag. It's a gift."

"I don't need a gift," Rachel said, her frustration growing. "Just stop."

He paid for the quilt and then tucked the bag under his arm and strode out of the shop. Rachel looked at Sylvia, baffled at what had transpired.

"Enjoy your quilt," the shopkeeper said.

She found Dermot standing on the sidewalk, his shoulders tense, his expression cloudy. His mood had turned so suddenly and Rachel couldn't figure out why. "I'm sorry," she said. "I didn't mean to seem ungrateful. I'm just used to buying quilts on my own."

"No. I'm sorry. I shouldn't have gotten so mad. I was just— I shouldn't have snapped."

Rachel stood beside him, staring out at the traffic on the street. "Why did you get mad?"

"You said that another quilt would come along. You wanted this one, but you were willing to let it go, knowing that another one would come along. Do you think you'd ever regret letting this one go?"

"Maybe. But it's just a quilt. And usually a better one comes—" Suddenly, Rachel realized what he was angry about. She groaned inwardly. "So at first men were donkeys and then they were sofas. And now they're quilts?"

"When you say it like that, it sounds really stupid," Dermot said. "I guess I'm just a little…sensitive." He laughed. "Shit, I can't believe I just said that. I'm not sensitive."

"You are not a quilt," she said. "I'm not going to throw you aside for another man…or quilt."

"I won't be here. Another quilt will come along. Like that Danny guy at the fair. Has he called yet?"

Rachel winced. He had called. And emailed twice. She'd put him off, but had decided to accept a lunch invitation after Dermot left. "He's not you."

"But he'll become me, once I'm gone. He's called, hasn't he?"

"Yes. But I don't have any plans to go out with him. Maybe we'll meet for lunch, but we're not going on a date. We're just friends."

"That's how we started," Dermot muttered.

"No, we started as lovers. And then we became friends."

He walked off down the street and Rachel followed after him. She'd never seen him like this, so on edge, so frustrated. Dermot had always taken things lightly. And now he'd gotten upset buying a quilt? Maybe saying goodbye was going to be a lot more difficult that she'd anticipated.

Rachel slipped her hand around his arm as he walked, falling into stride next to him. "Can you just slow down for a second? So we can talk?"

"I'd rather not discuss this. I feel kind of foolish right now." He stopped and held out the bag. "Here. I bought this for you. I want you to have it. Enjoy it. And please forget the conversation that came with it."

Rachel pasted a bright smile on her face. "A gift?" she cooed. "You bought me a gift." She examined the bag. "What could it possibly be?"

"All right, let's not ignore the fact that I temporarily flipped out. I've just been thinking about next week and how hard it's going to be to leave. And we haven't really talked about it. And I didn't think I was a jealous guy, but the thought of you just moving on to someone else irritates the hell out of me."

"I understand," Rachel said.

"You're beautiful and funny and exciting and I just think that someone is going to notice that and you're going to find some guy and fall madly in love and—"

"Who says I couldn't fall madly in love with you?" she asked.

"Could you?"

Rachel nodded. She'd already fallen, and pretty hard at that. But she wasn't quite sure she wanted to admit it. Yet. "What about you? Could you fall in love with me?"

Dermot nodded. "I think I could." He handed her the quilt. "I want you to have this. I want you to remember who bought it for you. And no matter what happens between us, when you look at it, you'll think of me. And maybe if you sleep under it, you'll dream of me." He laughed. "Strike that last part. That was horribly cheesy."

"I thought it was kind of romantic," Rachel said.

"I don't know what's wrong with me."

They started off down the street, the mood lighter, their argument forgotten. But Rachel couldn't help but speculate over his strange behavior. Dermot was usually so smooth, so charming. Everything that came out of his mouth was carefully crafted to make her feel beautiful and important. And now, suddenly, he was stumbling all over himself to express his feelings.

Maybe he was falling in love, Rachel mused. Or maybe he was in love already. She drew a long, slow breath. If that was true, then everything had just become a lot more complicated.

8

BY THE TIME DERMOT finished his shower, he was ready to relax. He and Rachel had spent the entire afternoon doing a health check on the herd, a tedious process that required looking over every goat, trimming hooves and checking ears and general health in preparation for breeding.

Since Trevor had decided to join the football team, he stayed after school every afternoon, joining the milking tasks an hour late. After the milking was done, the boys and Dermot cleaned the parlor and the shed and brought in fresh straw, while Rachel went back to the house to start dinner.

Dermot slipped his bare feet into his shoes and wandered out onto the porch, his unbuttoned shirt flapping in the warm breeze. He expected to find her sitting on the steps, a spot that had become "their place" to watch the sunset.

The boys were at the table doing their homework. "Do you know where Rachel is?" he asked.

"She said she had to go out to the barn," Taylor said.

Dermot jogged down the steps, happy to find that they'd have a few more moments alone. They'd fallen into a schedule of sorts over the past four days. Like any ordinary family there was a lot of juggling that went on, but it all seemed to work.

He looked for her in the office in the milking parlor and then walked through the goat barn. He found her sitting in a pile of straw next to Lady, the matriarch of the herd. A cluster of goats stood nearby, watching her.

"Hey," he called. "What's taking so long? I thought you'd be finished by now."

She turned to look at him and Dermot frowned. Tears were streaming down her cheeks. He hurried over to her and bent down. "Is she sick?" he said. "I'll call the vet."

"No, no." Rachel shook her head. "She's fine."

He sat down beside her. "What's wrong, then?"

Rachel drew a ragged breath. "I'm just getting sentimental. It's time to stop breeding her. She's got arthritis in her knees and she had a difficult birth last year. And she's starting to dry off already. So, her days as a dairy goat are over."

"What happens then?"

"She just gets to relax. She's given birth to twenty-two kids. She's a wonderful mother. I remember when she was born. It was the year before I graduated from high school. She was the last nanny I showed at the fair before I left for art school." A fresh round of tears started. "God, I'm getting so old."

"How old are you?"

"Twenty-five. How old are you?"

"Twenty-seven."

"We're both old."

"How long do goats usually live?"

"These goats live eleven or twelve years." She glanced over at the goats gathered nearby and shook her head. "I used to be so much better about this. I don't know why I'm suddenly so emotional."

Fresh tears trickled down her cheeks and she brushed them away impatiently. Dermot wrapped his arm around her shoulder and pulled her into his lap, cradling her as she wept. Smoothing his hand over her tangled hair, he whispered soft words to soothe her, and after a while, her sobs subsided.

"It's not about the goats," he said.

She looked up at him. "What?"

"I don't think you're crying about the goats."

She sniffled. "I don't want to talk about it."

He nodded, burying his face in her hair and kissing the top of her head. Dermot knew how she felt. With every day that passed, they came closer and closer to the time he'd have to leave. He'd looked at the bus ticket at least four or five times each day, just to remind himself that his stay here was almost over.

He'd thought about calling his grandfather and telling him that he'd found a brand-new life on Rachel's farm. But he was reluctant to make such a big decision without returning home first. He'd been living a fantasy life here. Everything had been so perfect that he had a hard time believing it was real.

The ache in his heart was real. The emotions he felt every time he touched her were more than real. So what was holding him back? She'd made it clear that there were feelings on her side. But how did he know if they'd last? Was he willing to give up his entire life in Seattle for just a chance at a future with Rachel?

He glanced around at the goats in the barn. Over the past five weeks, he'd grown to know them, too, their personalities, their silly idiosyncrasies. The kids were his favorites, little bundles of energy, always looking for trouble.

"You know, with the boys here and Eddie to take care of the goats, maybe you could get away for a week. We could go on a vacation together. Some warm place with white sand beaches and fruity drinks?"

"We stop milking sometime around the end of December."

Dermot frowned. "You just stop?"

"Well, two months before the kids are due, we stop milking the pregnant goats, which is usually most of them by that time. Then we only milk them once a day for two months after their kids are born. So things sort of slow down for a while before kidding starts."

"So you will have time off?"

"Yeah. Except that we won't have any income coming in. And the goats still have to be fed and—"

"It would be my treat," he said.

Rachel shook her head. "I couldn't do that."

"Why not? People do it all the time. We could call it a Christmas gift or a birthday gift or—"

"Have you ever taken a woman on vacation and paid for everything?"

Dermot opened his mouth, then snapped it shut again. "No. But I've never known a woman I wanted to spend my vacation with until I met you. Just promise me you'll consider it."

It was strange to imagine a moment when he wouldn't be able to reach out and touch her. Dermot had learned so much during his time with Rachel, about life, about love. He'd watched the sun rise and set, the season change. And he'd never felt more alive—or more vulnerable. Could he go back to a life that revolved around selling very rich people a yacht that they probably didn't need anyway?

It all seemed so dull and unimportant compared to the work he'd been doing for Rachel. Almost like a game. In truth, there were times in the past when he felt like a con man, when he knew he was selling a boat simply because the buyer was seeking a status symbol and not a sailboat. But it was all good money, so he never questioned anyone's motives.

He was good at his job, but was his job good for him? The more he thought about it, the more he began to wonder. Suddenly, working at Quinn Yachtworks didn't seem to mean so much. It wasn't who he was. It was just a job.

Rachel shifted in his arms and he looked down at her. She'd turned her face up to his and Dermot dropped a kiss on her lips. "Better?"

She nodded. "Yeah."

"Lady is a very special goat."

Rachel crawled out of his arms, then squatted down next to Lady and patted her. The goat shook her head, the bell around her neck clanking. "You're still the head mama, even if you won't have any more babies. Enjoy your retirement, Lady Belle."

She walked through the goats and stood in the doorway to the barnyard, the setting sun illuminating her face. Dermot crossed to stand behind her, wrapping his arms around her waist, his chin resting on her shoulder.

"Come on, let's go back to the house. I'll make you a nice hot bath and we'll have a glass of wine and relax."

They walked across the yard, his arm wrapped around her shoulders. The boys had finished their homework and were throwing a football around in the waning light, Benny running back and forth, trying to play with them. When they got inside, Dermot took her upstairs and gently undressed her, then filled the tub with hot water.

When she was settled, he sat down beside the tub and grabbed the sponge. Once it was lathered, he scrubbed her back, brushing aside her hair. "It's been a good day," he said.

"It has. And it's nice having you here with me at the end of it all." She braced her arms on the edge of the old tub and looked up at him. "Thank you."

Cupping her face in his hands, Dermot kissed her softly. "No problem."

"You know, you've been a really important part of this farm these last weeks. And worth a whole lot more than a hundred dollars a week."

"How much am I worth?" he asked with a playful smile.

"A million dollars," she said.

"That much?"

"I wish I had enough money to lure you away from your regular job."

"That wouldn't take money," he said.

Dermot thought about what it would take. He'd considered staying, making a life with Rachel. It was easy to believe that what he shared with her was real and lasting. But he had a life somewhere else. Did he love her simply because she needed him?

"I'm going to go down and get you a glass of

wine," he said. "And then, I'm going to wash your hair for you."

Rachel sank down in the water and closed her eyes. "Two million," she said. "That's what you're worth."

Dermot walked downstairs, and when he got to the kitchen, he stood in front of the fridge and stared inside, his thoughts occupied with the woman upstairs. Every ounce of common sense told him that he'd have to go. At least for a little while. How would he ever know if their feelings for each other were true unless he had a chance to put them in perspective? With Rachel in his arms and in his bed, he'd been lost in an infatuation that didn't seem to have an end.

He drew a deep breath and let it out slowly. Women had always held a very specific place in his life. He'd never, ever let any woman get under his skin like Rachel had. She'd become a part of who he was as a man, and excising her from his life would be like losing an arm or a leg.

If he were at home, he'd go out for a beer with his brothers and they'd be able to give him some solid advice. But he felt more than just a physical distance from them. The bonds that had seemed so strong between the four of them had been replaced by the bond he shared with Rachel.

He reached for the bottle of wine and then closed the refrigerator. Drawing a deep breath, he fixed his mind on the naked woman upstairs. If he thought about the future, he got lost in a vortex of confusion.

He'd just have to take one day at a time and hope that, when it came to goodbyes, he'd know exactly what to do.

ON WARM NIGHTS, they ate dinner on the porch around a weathered wooden table with a bouquet of wild-flowers in the center. The boys had been at the farm for a week and were already settling into a happy routine.

Though their presence had put a bit of a crimp in her sex life, Rachel and Dermot had managed to find plenty of time together in the afternoons, before Taylor came home from school. But now they had Saturday and Sunday to contend with, and Rachel found herself planning a little getaway in the late-night hours.

"I'm starving," Dermot called through the screen door.

"Me, too," Taylor yelled.

"Me, three," added Trevor.

"So hungry that you'll even eat my cooking?" She stepped out onto the porch, her arms laden with plates and bowls. "Dinner is served."

"I love your cooking," Dermot said, grabbing a platter as she walked past. "Can't you tell? I think I've put on a few pounds since I got here."

"You're just being polite," she said. "I know I'm not a great cook."

He nuzzled her neck and she giggled, trying to

wriggle out of his embrace. "You're good enough for me."

"Thank you," she said, finally escaping his arms. She returned a moment later with a bottle of wine and two glasses, then handed them to Dermot before she sat down. The boys filled their plates and sat down on the porch steps, tossing bits of bread to Benny, who sat between them.

Dermot poured her a glass of wine. "I love your meatloaf." He chuckled. "And that was purely a non-sexual comment."

Rachel smiled and leaned over her plate to kiss him. "Stop it," she whispered.

"Are you finally ready to be rid of me?"

Rachel shook her head. "No. I'm going to be lonely without you."

"You could come with me," he said.

"No!" Taylor shouted. "She has to stay here. So do you."

They had carefully avoided talk of the future for the past few weeks. But in the past couple days, it seemed to come up again and again. "It was beautiful while it lasted," she murmured.

"Why haven't you asked me to stay?"

She was shocked by the question and she frowned, trying to read the expression on his face. Rachel had never even considered that he might be happy living on the farm with her. Sure, he felt a need to help her, but Dermot didn't seem like the kind of man to be happy tending goats for the rest of his life. "I—I guess I know how anxious you are to get home. Back to your brothers and your grandfather."

"*You* feel like my family," he said.

"That feeling will go away. You're tricked into that because we've been so close. We've been living like an old married couple." She nodded to the boys. "With two kids."

"I don't think that feeling's going to go away," he said, picking at his food.

The sound of a car on the gravel driveway interrupted their discussion and Rachel slowly stood, staring out into the yard. "Oh, no."

"What is it?" Dermot folded his napkin and set it on the table. "Who is it?"

"It's my brother. I should have known this was coming. He shows up every now and then to try to convince me to sell the farm. I've been ignoring the letters from the lawyers, which has probably pissed him off."

"He can't force you to sell the farm. It's in your father's will."

"That's not going to stop him," Rachel said. "And now that the boys are here, he knows his case is not so good anymore."

Dermot stood up and moved to her side, slipping his arm around her waist. She could feel his body tense beside her and she knew from the look on her brother's face that he had run out of patience.

"Why is Uncle Jim here?" Taylor asked. Trevor stood up as if he sensed the tension in the air.

"Guys, why don't you take your dinner inside," Dermot ordered. They reluctantly went into the house, but stood at the screen door, watching the scene unfold in front of them. Dermot grabbed Rachel's hand as they stood at the bottom of the porch steps.

"Hello, Jim," Rachel said as her brother strode up to them. "It's nice to see you."

"Rachel," he said with a curt nod. "I'd heard Jane's boys were living here."

"They are. This is Dermot. Dermot Quinn. He's my—"

"Boyfriend," Dermot interrupted.

"Boyfriend?" Jim's brow rose perceptively. She could tell that the news wasn't what he wanted to hear. A boyfriend meant help on the farm. The longer Rachel struggled on her own, the happier her siblings had been.

"Yes." She glanced up at Dermot. "My boyfriend. He lives here with me—and the boys. And Eddie."

"I do," Dermot said, forcing a smile.

"So things are going better than when I saw you last?"

She nodded. "Much better. The dairy is running smoothly. I'm thinking of increasing the size of the herd. We just had our state inspection a few weeks ago and passed with flying colors. The price of goat's milk is up, so I can't complain. Would you like to stay for supper? We're having meatloaf and mashed potatoes."

He shook his head. "I'm just on my way home. I had a business meeting in Madison and thought I'd check things out."

"I can give you a little tour," she said. "If you're interested."

Jim shook his head. "No, no. That's fine. I'm just going to head out." He turned for the car, then realized his manners. "It was nice meeting you…"

"Dermot." Dermot sent him one of his most charming smiles. "Nice meeting you, Jim. Drive safe, now."

Jim turned back to Rachel. "I don't know why you're doing this, but one day you're going to realize that you've wasted your life working on this farm. It would be better for all of us if you'd just give up gracefully."

"I'm not going to do that," she said.

Cursing beneath his breath, he walked away. She and Dermot watched as he turned the car around and roared out of the driveway, gravel spitting up from the tires. The boys rejoined them on the porch.

"Why did he come here?" Taylor asked.

"He just wanted to check up on me," Rachel explained.

"He wants Aunt Rachel to sell the farm," Trevor said. "Our mom wanted that, too, until she brought us here."

"I promised your grandfather that I would try to

keep the farm in the family," Rachel said. "And you boys are family. As long as you're here, we're not going to sell the farm." She smiled at them. "Don't worry. You have a home here for as long as you want."

They seemed to be relieved and Rachel felt good, knowing that they were becoming attached to their legacy. Maybe goat farming skipped a generation?

She and Dermot sat back down at the dinner table and continued to eat. He grabbed her hand and brought it to his lips, kissing it just below her wrist. "If you ever need help, if money gets tight and you're afraid you'll lose the farm, I want you to promise that you'll call me."

She smiled and gave him a hug. "Thank you, that's very—"

"It wouldn't need to be a loan. Call it an investment. You wouldn't have to pay me back. It would be like a timeshare. I could come and work the farm whenever I wanted and you wouldn't have to worry."

Rachel laughed at the notion. "A timeshare on a goat farm. Gee, I wonder if we could sell a whole bunch of shares? You're very funny."

"I've grown to love this place almost as much as you do. And I have plenty of money. And I am your boyfriend, after all."

"Thank you," she said, emotion filling her throat. "But I really think I need to do this on my own. If I can't make it work, then my brothers are right. I'm wasting my time."

Dermot pulled her into his embrace. "I just want you to be happy," he said. He kissed her, lingering over her mouth for a long time before stopping.

"I am happy," she said. "Right now, at this very moment, I don't think I've ever been happier."

"Then let's finish our dinner and watch the sun set and then go to bed."

"Separate beds," she whispered.

"I have a plan," Dermot said. "Do you want me to tell you about it?"

"I think we can save that for dessert," Rachel said softly.

"I thought we were having pie for dessert," Dermot said.

Rachel groaned. "Is that all you boys think about? Food?"

"Yes!" Trevor and Taylor shouted from the kitchen.

"No," Dermot murmured. "But it does take my mind off the other hungers."

A shiver skittered down her spine. "Behave," she warned.

DERMOT LAY ON HIS BED in the stone house. The weather had cooled and a breeze blew at the curtains, rustling the maple trees outside the window. He hadn't spent a night in this bed since his first one on the farm. But now, it was the only place he and Rachel could find any privacy when the boys were around.

He understood her reluctance to set a bad example.

They were affectionate with each other in front of the boys but when it came to sleeping in the same bedroom, Rachel drew the line. Dermot found that quite amusing, prude by day, wanton by night.

He heard the screen door downstairs squeak. And then soft footfalls on the stairs. Dermot sat up, waiting, listening, watching the door in the moonlight filtering through the bedroom window. And then, she was there, silhouetted in light and shadow, her long limbs visible beneath the thin fabric of her nightgown.

Dermot crawled off the bed and crossed the room, then pulled her into his arms. "I thought you'd never get here," he whispered. He ran his fingers through her hair and drew her into a long, deep kiss. "I've missed you."

"You just saw me a few hours ago," Rachel said.

"That's too long." Dermot scooped her up in his arms and carried her to the bed. He gently set her down, then braced his hands on either side of her, pushing her back until he was stretched out above her.

They were so familiar with each other that she knew exactly how to pleasure him. She reached down and caressed him through the soft fabric of his boxers. He was already growing hard and he felt an ache deep inside him, an overwhelming need to bury himself in her warmth. It was a sensation that he'd come to crave, that moment when he was settled deep inside her and before he began to move.

At that moment, he felt as if they were connected

in a way that could never be broken, that their bodies and souls had become one. Even though she'd soon be miles and miles away, he'd still be able recall how she felt, how she made him feel.

Desperate for that intimacy, he grabbed the hem of her nightgown and pulled it over her head, then tossed it on the floor. She was naked beneath, and when he reached out to caress her breast, Rachel arched against his touch, her breath escaping on a soft sigh.

He wanted to tease her slowly, bringing her to her release with his fingers and his tongue. But he felt a desperate need to possess her, to reassure himself nothing would ever change between them, and Dermot couldn't deny himself. His mouth found hers again as he shoved the boxers down over his hips. Slowly, he slipped inside her, and when he could penetrate no deeper, he froze. The sensations racing through his body were almost more than he could handle.

Tonight, they'd find their release together and it would be perfect. And when it was over, he'd tell himself once again that even though he didn't want to live without her, the feelings coursing through his body weren't love at all, just a by-product of passion.

Rachel shifted, pressing her lips to his shoulder. She gently bit his arm, grazing her teeth over his skin. He'd taught her what he liked, that mixture of plea-sure with a little pain, and she'd taken the lesson seriously. She'd taught him that she believed foreplay was for people with more patience than she possessed.

"Are you going to move?" she whispered.

"Do you want me to move?"

"Mmm." She wrapped her legs around his waist then rolled on top of him. "Or I could move. Let's try that."

She pushed up on her knees, then drove down on top of him. Dermot gasped. "Maybe we shouldn't do that. This will be over before you realize it."

"You're not trying hard enough," Rachel teased. "Just think of something else."

"Sweetheart, when you're naked in my arms, it's impossible to think of anything else."

Rachel smiled down at him, her pale hair falling in waves around her face. She bent close and kissed him, her tongue teasing at his. Though they'd probably made love fifty times, it was never the same. Each encounter revealed some new passion or hidden desire.

As she began to move again, Dermot grasped her hips, trying to slow her pace. But Rachel seemed determined to challenge his control with every stroke and every sigh, pushing him closer and closer to the edge.

She closed her eyes and pressed her palms to his chest, her expression a mix of intensity and exhilaration. He wanted to touch her, to help her find her release, but when he tried, she brushed his hand away.

When he felt her pace increase, there was nothing more he could do to stave off his orgasm. Suddenly, Rachel stopped, her body arching against his, her fingers digging into his shoulders. And then she dissolved into shudders and spasms, her breath coming in gasps as she cried out.

The moment he felt her body convulse around him, Dermot knew he was lost. He grabbed her waist and rolled her beneath him. Reality fell out of focus and he let the waves wash over him, every nerve in his body firing, every tension releasing.

It was over so quickly. Dermot curled up beside her, his leg thrown across her hips. "How the hell am I supposed to get along without that?"

"There's always self-gratification," Rachel said. She looked over at him. "We could do it over the phone."

"Or the computer."

"I will miss you," Rachel said, nuzzling her face into his shoulder.

"What will you miss the most?" Dermot asked.

She pushed up on her elbow, her hand smoothing over his chest. "I'm not sure I could name just one thing. It's a lot of really strange things, things I just started noticing. Like when you eat cereal in the morning, you turn your bowl after each bite. And when you sleep, you just throw yourself all over the bed, like a giant rag doll. And the goats seem to like you a lot more than they like me." Rachel curled back up beside him. "What about me? What will you miss the most?"

"This," he said.

"Sex?"

"No," Dermot replied. "This. Just you and me. All alone, listening to you talk. Knowing I can just pull you into my arms and kiss you or make love to you."

Rachel rolled over and folded her arms across her chest. "I want you to leave your clothes here with me."

"You want my clothes?"

She nodded. "They smell like you. I can sleep with them until I get used to you being gone. Kind of like a security blanket." She reached over and grabbed his pillow and pulled it to her. "I think I'll take this with me for now."

"Where are you going?"

"I should go back to my own room. In case the boys get up and need something."

"Stay," he said. "We have so little time left. We'll just get up before they do. I always wake up in time. I promise, they won't even know you're gone."

The breeze freshened and a cool wind blew through the bedroom. Rachel reached down and pulled the old quilt up around them both. "Did you feel that?"

"Yeah."

"Autumn is coming. We'll breed the goats and watch them all get round and lazy. And then, starting sometime in February, they'll all have babies.

Even though it's the dead of winter, it's my favorite time of the year."

As his hands smoothed over her hips, he couldn't help but feel a surge of need. Would there ever come a time when he didn't want her? When they'd completely exhausted their desire for each other? The prospect of waking up alone, without her beside him, was almost unimaginable. Casual sex with any other woman would never satisfy him again.

Raking his fingers through his hair, Dermot closed his eyes. He felt her palm move to his face.

It should be easy to rationalize the end of their time together, Dermot mused. He'd walked away from any number of women with whom he'd shared longer relationships. But it wasn't just the physical uncoupling that he found difficult. From the beginning he'd been attached to Rachel emotionally, and that bond had only strengthened over the past weeks.

Even now, the thought of letting her go caused an ache deep inside of him, an emptiness that couldn't be filled, not even with another woman. The kind of pleasure that he'd experienced with Rachel had been unique and perfect and it would be impossible to find with anyone else.

Dermot closed his eyes and drew a deep breath. He would get over her and he'd learn to live without her. It was just a matter of letting go.

9

Rachel sat on the end of the bed, watching as Dermot packed the last of his clothes in his leather duffel. He remembered the day he'd stepped off the bus in Mapleton, wondering what he was supposed to do with himself for six weeks. And now, time had flown so quickly, it seemed like just yesterday that he'd met her outside the feed store.

"What time does your bus leave?" she asked.

"4:00 p.m."

He'd said goodbye to the boys before they left for school and later had a long talk with Eddie about the future and "carpe"ing his diem. And then, he'd walked through the barn and said his farewells to the goats.

He and Rachel had spent the early afternoon in her bed, curled up with each other, talking about the time they'd spent together. It was as if he was about to wander into a deep desert and she was the last drop of water he'd have. She was sweet and satisfying. And like water, she was what kept him alive.

"How long will it take for you to get home?"

"A while," he said. "The ride out here was two days and four transfers."

"You had enough for a plane ticket," she said. "Before you bought that quilt. Why don't you let me buy you a plane ticket?"

He'd never thought of that option. It would give him two extra days to spend with Rachel. But his grandfather had given all four of them very specific instructions. And two and a half days of nothing but passing scenery would give him time to sort out everything that had happened in the past six weeks.

He sighed softly. He'd thought his grandfather had gone off the deep end with this plan of his. When he'd left Seattle, Dermot couldn't imagine any other life for himself but the one he had. And now, he was forced to admit that the life he'd shared with Rachel was…perfect. Wonderful. A revelation.

"I have to take the bus," he said. "It's part of the deal."

"Are you excited to get back?" she asked.

"No," he said. "I mean, I'm looking forward to seeing my brothers. I'd love to know what they've been up to. But after living here on the farm, my life at home seems a bit dull."

She giggled. "You think the farm is more exciting than living in Seattle?"

"I've loved this life," he said. "It's simple and oddly satisfying. I've loved working beside you and sitting at the table watching you make dinner and I even love burning the garbage. I feel healthy, like I've actually put in a day's work when I'm done." He held out his hands. "And I have calluses."

"I'm sorry," she said, reaching out to take his hands in hers.

"For what? They're like a badge of honor."

He slipped his hand around her nape, then she pulled him down on the bed with her. "I can't imagine what would have happened if my grandfather had handed me a different ticket. I would never have met you."

"Maybe I would have hired one of your brothers?"

"Maybe," he said. But the thought of Rachel with any other man but him was difficult to tolerate. "No. I don't think so."

"How do you know?" she asked. "If they look anything like you, I might have."

"Actually, they all look a lot like me." He ran his hand down to her breast, cupping the warm flesh in his palm. "But none of this would have happened."

"How do you know?"

He bent close, his breath warm on her ear. "Because you were made for me, and me alone," he whispered.

She wrapped her arms around his neck and gave him a fierce kiss. "It's like we know each other so well. But we only know us. We don't know anything else. Just what's gone on between us."

"This is all that makes any difference," Dermot said. "And the other stuff, we'll learn later."

"Later? When is later? Not tomorrow, or next week. We're all out of time."

He sat up next to her. "We don't have to be, Rachel. We can find a way to be together. We just have to figure it out."

"I can't ask you to stay," she said.

"And I won't ask you to leave," he countered.

"Then where does that leave us?"

He smoothed his hand across her cheek. "Maybe you'll decide to leave. Or maybe I'll decide to come back. You never know what might happen."

She nodded slowly. "You never know." Rachel lay back down and stared at the ceiling of her bedroom. "Tell me what you're going to do when you get home. I want to imagine you there."

"First, I'll probably lie down on my sofa. It's a really nice leather sofa. And I'll turn on the game. I get home on a Sunday, so that means football. Hopefully, the Seahawks will be playing. I'll have a beer, take a shower and then at about five, my time, I'll call you and we'll spend the rest of the night on the phone."

"That would be nice," she said.

"And then I'll talk to you through Skype and we can actually see each other."

"That would be even better," she said.

"This isn't the end, Rachel. Not by a long shot." He pressed his forehead to hers. "You believe that, don't you?"

"I think I do."

He kissed her. "Good." Dermot drew a deep breath. "We should probably go. I don't want to miss my bus."

"It's not due for another hour," she said.

"If we don't leave now, I'm going to take off all my clothes and all of your clothes and we're going to lose all track of time."

Rachel stood up and held out her hand. "All right. Let's go."

Dermot grabbed his bag and followed her out. Eddie was sitting on the porch of the old stone house. He waved and Benny came running up, looking for a treat. Dermot gave him a pat on the head before Rachel handed him the keys. He helped her into the passenger side. When he got behind the wheel, she was staring at him.

"What?"

"You know, I never even took a photo of you. We should have taken some photos."

"I guess we were too busy with other activities," he said.

"Promise you'll send me one? Take one outside your house. Take lots of pictures of your house and your office, so I can imagine you there. And take a picture of your bed, too."

"So you can imagine me there?"

"No, so I can imagine myself there with you," she said.

He reached over and wove his fingers through the soft hair at her temple. "I think I can do that."

The rest of the ride into town passed in silence, both of them lost in their own thoughts. He wanted to say so many things to her, to tell her how much she meant to him, to tell her that he was falling in love with her. But the more he said, the more complicated his leaving became.

And yet, why was he holding back now? He had a chance to change the course of his life, to capture the heart of the most incredible woman he'd ever met. Yet, he couldn't gather the courage to put himself out there, to risk rejection, to expose his vulnerabilities.

Why couldn't she say it first? Just so he knew that she felt the same way. Dermot thought he saw it in her face, in the way she looked at him. But he'd never been in love before, so it was difficult to know if he was reading the signs right.

By the time they reached town, he'd twisted himself into so many knots that he wasn't sure where he stood with Rachel. He pulled up in front of the bus stop and they both hopped out of the truck. Rachel opened the tailgate and they sat on it, dangling their legs.

"Are you going to wait here with me?" he asked.

"I am. I'm going to spend every last moment with you that I can."

"You're not going to cry, are you? Because if you cry, I don't know what I'm going to do."

"You can kiss me and tell me everything will be all right. And that we'll see each other again soon." She drew a ragged breath. "But I'm not going to cry. I think if I start, I won't be able to stop."

"Please don't cry," he murmured. He bent close and kissed her. Even after all this time, the temptation to touch her was more than he could resist. He'd grown so used to having complete freedom around her, to act on his affections and his needs. "I don't want that to be the thing I'm thinking of all the way to Seattle."

"All right," she said. "You'll kiss me goodbye and that will be it." She glanced at her watch. "We have some time yet. Why don't we go inside and get a bite to eat? Then I won't have to sit at the dinner table tonight, missing you."

The town's café served as the bus station, and before they got a table, he rechecked the schedule. Dermot ordered a large coffee and two ham sandwiches to go, and Rachel ordered a slice of pie. They shared the pie in a booth at the window, teasing and joking with each other in an attempt to alleviate the emotion between them.

When the bus pulled up in front of the café, Dermot reached out and took her hand, then pressed his lips to her fingers. Then they both got up and walked outside, her hand in his. Dermot was almost afraid to let her go, afraid that by doing so, the connection between them would be broken forever.

The bus driver looked at them. "Are you both traveling today?"

Dermot shook his head. "Just me."

"Can I stow your bag?"

He shook his head. "I'll carry it." He turned back to Rachel. "So, I guess this is it. You'll be all right on your own?"

She nodded, gently untangling her fingers from his. "I will. Don't worry."

He bent close, then pulled her body against his and kissed her. What began as a frantic meeting of lips and tongues softened into a kiss filled with longing and regret. Suddenly, he didn't want to leave anything unsaid. He needed her to know exactly how he felt. "I love you, Rachel."

She looked up at him with a wide-eyed gaze. "I—I love you, too." She threw her arms around his neck. "I do."

Dermot grinned, then kissed her again. "Good. I'm glad we have that settled."

"Have a safe trip. And call me when you get home."

He kissed her once more, then turned and walked onto the bus. When he found an empty seat, he looked out the window to find her watching him. Rachel blew him a kiss, then gave him a little wave as the bus pulled away from the curb.

Dermot watched her as long as he could, looking over the back of his seat to see the last glimpse of her through the rear window of the bus. When there was no longer anything more to see, he sat down again, leaning back in his seat and closing his eyes.

With every mile that passed, the ache grew a bit deeper. It was as if his heart was being torn out of him, one molecule at a time. Dermot wasn't sure there would be anything left of it when he got back to Seattle.

He loved her. There was no doubt in his mind. And though Dermot wasn't sure how it had happened, he'd managed to find the one woman in the world who could make him blissfully happy. And he was on a bus, driving in the opposite direction.

"No one ever said you were the smartest guy on the planet," he muttered to himself.

RACHEL STARED AT THE PHOTO that Dermot had sent her, the image smiling out at her from her laptop screen. He was standing in front of his house with a silly looking cheesehead hat on his head. He'd obviously spent a few of his hard-earned dollars on a memento before he got across the state line.

He was so handsome. Even after a month apart, she could still remember every detail of the time they'd spent together. They spoke every day, sometimes two or three times, over video chat on her computer. At night, before she fell asleep, they talked about their day, Rachel recounting everything that had happened on the farm.

Without the ability to be distracted by physical pleasures, they were getting to know much more about each other. Most of the questions she'd had about his life in Seattle had been answered and discussed in great detail. She'd learned the full story of his parents' death, about their childhood before and after they became orphans.

She learned that his grandfather had come from a tiny fishing village on Bantry Bay in Ireland and that Martin Quinn had been a widower with a son when he arrived in the U.S.

She fell asleep to his handsome face and watched him sleep in the early hours of the morning when she got up. It was almost like having him with her again. But the daily routine on the farm had become far less exciting without him there to talk to her, to help her with the work.

The boys had more than made up for his absence when it came to the farm work. For some odd reason, they seemed to delight in the early mornings in the barn. And the moment they got home from school, they were back at work, Eddie now advising them on the proper way to do things.

After a late dinner, Trevor and Taylor did homework at the kitchen table, then were off to bed by nine. Rachel kept asking if they wanted to go into town to hang out with friends, but they seemed to be most comfortable with each other. Dermot had told her that the bonds between brothers were strong and she was seeing it firsthand with her nephews. Still stinging from the upset in their living arrangements and the breakup of their parents' marriage, they were wary of strangers.

Still, they had found a few things of interest at school. They'd both joined the chess club and the math team. And Trevor was still playing on the junior varsity football team, staying late for practice every night after school. Once football was over, they planned to join 4-H so they could learn more about showing goats at the fair.

Rachel didn't have the heart to tell them that they might not be at the farm next summer for the county fair. They needed to know that they had found a permanent home for as long as their mother wanted them living at Clover Meadow.

At least Rachel's life had become more interesting. She'd baked cookies for a booster club bake sale and she'd cheered Trevor on from the stands at the game. But she couldn't help but feel that her life was incomplete without Dermot.

There was a big empty spot in her heart where he'd once resided. And though they spoke every day, she felt the overwhelming need to touch him and kiss him, to crawl into bed naked and make love to him.

Home was supposed to be where she was happy. And the only way she could be happy now was if she were here with Dermot. And since he wasn't on the farm with her, the farm didn't feel like home anymore. Rachel closed her eyes and tried to remember when Dermot was with her, when they had all the time in the world together. Six weeks didn't seem long enough, and yet it was all she'd needed to fall hopelessly in love with him.

Rachel stood up and carried her plate to the kitchen and rinsed it off. Closing her eyes, she braced her hands on the edge of the counter and drew a deep breath. The screen door squeaked and she felt a flutter in her stomach.

How long would it take before she realized that he wasn't the one entering the kitchen? She turned around, ready to greet the boys arriving home from school, then realized they were fifteen minutes early. Instead she found her sister, Jane, standing at the door. Her face was haggard and she had deep shadows beneath her eyes. She looked as if she was ready to collapse from the effort of holding her suitcases.

"Hi," Rachel said. "What are you doing here?"

Jane set the suitcases down on the floor and looked up, her eyes filling with tears. "I— I'm—" She wiped the tears away and forced a smile. "Sorry, I was just—" A sob tore from her throat.

Rachel crossed the room and gathered her in her arms, rubbing her hand across her sister's back. Jane had always been thin, but Rachel could feel bones beneath her starched white blouse. "Don't worry. It's going to be all right. You're home now. Everything will be fine."

Rachel gently moved Jane to a chair and sat her down, then took the place next to her at the table. Holding her hand, she tried to soothe her weeping.

"I don't know why I'm crying now," Jane said. "I haven't allowed myself any tears, even when he told me about the affair. I've been a freaking rock."

"It's because you feel safe here," Rachel said.

She glanced around. "Where are the boys? I don't want them to see me crying."

"They'll be home soon. Trevor has a game tonight. He's going to be so excited that you're here."

"He told me about the football team," she said. "Rachel, I can't thank you enough for doing this. You've spared them so much heartache letting them live here."

Rachel took her hand and gave it a squeeze. "They know what's going on."

"You told them?"

"No, they told me. They're aware of a whole lot more than you give them credit for. And we've talked. I've been honest. And they're confused, but they know this doesn't have anything to do with them. And they're worried about you. And really angry with their father."

Jane threw her arms around Rachel's neck and

gave her a hug. "I know I don't deserve your help after the way I've treated you. About the will and the farm. And I'm so glad you didn't sell. The boys and I would be homeless now if you had." She drew a deep breath. "And I'm going to do everything I can to help out around here."

"You're going to stay?"

Jane nodded. "I—I've been thinking that this might be a good place to raise my boys. I mean, they seem to like it here and—"

"They love it here," Rachel said. "And they love working the farm. They want to join 4-H and they're starting to make some friends at school."

"You were right to keep the place," Jane said.

"I think I was." She shrugged. "I was kind of lonely here at first, but now there's a whole family living here."

"What about that guy, the one I met when I dropped the boys off? What was his name?"

"Dermot." Rachel drew a ragged breath. "He's gone. Back to Seattle. We still talk every day, but it's been impossible to get together. He's really busy with work and I can't leave the farm right now."

"But you can soon. I'm here now. I'm going to learn everything about raising goats." Jane sighed. "It's all right that I'm here, isn't it?"

Rachel nodded. "It's your home, too. And I think Dad would be happy that you and the boys are here. He talked about them a lot."

"I've been so…selfish. I should have brought them to see him when he was sick. I just didn't think he'd… well, I thought he was going to live forever. Nothing is forever. I guess I've learned that."

A rumble sounded from outside. "The bus is here," Rachel said. "Why don't you go say hello to your boys. I'll make something for them to eat. I can't tell you how much Trevor and Taylor eat. They have a meal when they get home from school and then another after milking is finished and then another before they go to bed."

Jane stood up. "Well, I'm here and I'm going to start contributing. I'm getting the proceeds from our house to use for child support until their father can start paying. It should keep us going for a while."

As she watched her sister run out the door, Rachel felt as if a great weight had been lifted off her shoulders. If Jane was really serious about staying, then Rachel could have her own life and keep her promise to her father. She felt a surge of emotion as she thought of his pride that his grandsons might one day run the farm he'd loved so much.

She walked to the back door and stepped out onto the porch, watching the scene unfold at the end of the driveway. Her sister met the boys with her arms outstretched, then gathered them both into a hug, laughing and crying at the same time.

Rachel felt tears threaten and imagined how it would feel the next time she saw Dermot. Would she throw herself into his arms? Would she cry happy tears? For the first time since he'd left, she'd begun to believe there might be a chance for them.

"Soon," she murmured. "Soon."

The boys hurried down the drive, then dropped their backpacks on the porch before heading to the barn, their mother in tow. "Hey, change your clothes before you start working," Rachel called. "And, Trevor, you need to come in and eat early if you've got a game tonight."

"We just want to show Mom the goats," Taylor said. "We'll be right back."

"Don't go out into the barnyard with your school shoes," Rachel warned.

Jane turned and smiled at her, then mouthed a thank-you. She slipped her arms around her sons' shoulders and headed across the yard to the barn.

Rachel rubbed her arms against the chill in the air, then turned and walked back inside. The responsibility of parenting the boys had injected a lot of worry into her day-to-day life. But now that Jane was here, she could relax a bit.

The experience hadn't been all that difficult. In fact, she'd been able to see that she might not make a bad parent one day. But part of her success had come from Dermot's insights. From the moment the boys had arrived on the farm, he'd taken them both under his wing.

She grabbed the bread from the refrigerator and

began to assemble three ham sandwiches, the favorite pre-dinner dinner for the boys. They'd find the milk and cookies on their own.

She had an hour before milking, and after that, they'd go into town for Trevor's football game. Right now, she wanted to curl up in bed and talk to Dermot. She grabbed her laptop from the table, unplugging the power cord.

To her delight, the boys had put in a wireless router to handle the three laptops in the house. It allowed her to talk to Dermot from anywhere, including the barn. Rachel climbed the stairs and shut her bedroom door behind her. Then she opened her laptop and dialed into Dermot's computer. A few seconds later his face appeared on the screen.

"You're early," he said. "Is everything all right?

"It's fine," she said. "I just wanted to hear your voice."

"Are you in your bedroom?" Dermot asked.

"Yes."

"Are you naked?"

"No," Rachel said. "But I can take care of that if you want."

He groaned. "We have to stop with the online sex, sweetheart. It's making me crazy."

Rachel smiled. "I thought we were getting rather good at it."

"It's not like the real thing," Dermot replied.

"Why don't you take off your clothes first," she said.

"I can't right now. I'm at the office and I have a meeting in exactly three minutes. But we can make a date for later."

"I'm going to Trevor's football game later. And Jane is here now, so I have to get her settled. But I will try."

"I'll be waiting," he said. He kissed his fingertips and pressed them to the screen. "Miss you."

"I miss you more," Rachel said.

She pressed her fingers to the screen. A moment later, it went black and she sighed softly. How many more nights would she have to spend alone?

DERMOT SAT AT A STOPLIGHT, the Mercedes sedan idling beneath the music coming from the radio. The wipers slapped back and forth in a counter-tempo and he squinted out into the afternoon shower.

His mind flashed back to the rainy afternoons he'd spent on Rachel's farm, the quiet time making love in her bed while the thunder rumbled outside, the freshened air blowing at the lace curtains in her bedroom.

All of his memories were so clear, so real, that he could almost imagine himself back there. He knew they'd agreed to wait until Christmas before they saw each other again, but every weekend, after every call, he fought the urge to hop on a plane and go visit her.

He couldn't imagine that she'd be disappointed

to see him. They spent every evening on the phone or on video chat, and though it wasn't even close to being enough, it was all he had for now.

How many nights had he lain awake, thinking about making love to her, reliving every moment they'd spent in each other's arms. It wasn't just the miles between them, it was the need to touch her, to reassure himself that she was real, that what they'd shared was real.

He thought that returning to Seattle would help him put his priorities in order. But since he and his brothers had returned, everything had been turned upside down. All four of them had managed to meet women who had changed their lives, but none of them had made a move to leave Seattle for love.

It didn't help that in the six weeks away, work had piled up and they were busier than they'd ever been. Dermot had three sales trips planned for the next two weeks, all to meet clients who were looking to build a custom yacht.

He used to love his job, the challenge of the sale, the high he got when a client signed on the bottom line and handed over a check for the down payment. And it had been fun to socialize with the rich and famous. It had certainly put him in a good place to meet a lot of beautiful women.

But there was only one woman he was interested in now and she was living on a farm in Wisconsin, tending to a herd of troublesome goats. Dermot smiled as he remembered the two of them, standing on the gate and watching as the goats frolicked in the field.

This was crazy. Why was he denying himself the only thing that he really wanted in the world? The truth was, he was just marking time here in Seattle, waiting until he could see her again. Why not just go?

Dermot picked up his cell phone and dialed his office number. His assistant picked up after two rings. "Hey, Lisa. I need you to book me a ticket for Chicago, for tonight. See if you can find a flight that leaves after seven. I still have to get through rush hour and get home to pack. Eight would be even better. And reserve a rental car."

He finished giving her the details, then hung up. A slow smile broke across his face. "That was easy," he murmured to himself. Now, should he tell Rachel he was coming or should it be a surprise? They usually did a video chat around six his time and she'd be expecting that. But he could do that from the airport, if need be.

Given the travel time between Chicago and Seattle, and the drive out to the farm, he'd probably arrive in the middle of the night. He'd call her when he was a few miles away.

His phone rang and he picked it up. The caller ID was from Lisa in the office. "Are we booked?" he asked.

"Sorry," she said. "There are no seats left on any flights direct from Sea-Tac to Chicago. If you want to fly to L.A. first, I can get you to Chicago by 5:00 a.m. Or you can fly to Atlanta and then to Chicago, but that puts you in really late, too. You can go to the airport and wait to see if something opens up."

"No," Dermot said. "Never mind. I'll try to book something for next weekend. Take a look at the schedules for me and find some good flights."

He sighed softly as he waited for the traffic to start moving again. If he hadn't scheduled a sales appointment in Tacoma for late in the day, he would have been home by now, enjoying a cold beer and ordering a pizza.

He'd gone back to his normal eating habits since returning from Wisconsin. Farm work had kept him incredibly fit and even the huge breakfasts and crazy fair food hadn't impacted his waist. But once he returned to his sedentary life in Seattle, he'd had to work hard to keep fit.

There were days when he longed for the deep, exhausting exercise that he got loading straw and feed bags into the back of the truck, and muscling goats into the milking stanchions. It was hard work, but it had been satisfying.

And yet, he knew he couldn't live on the farm with Rachel. As much as he loved her, for now, his place was here with his grandfather and his brothers. They'd both been trapped by family loyalty, Rachel in her quest to keep the farm in the family and him in his need to pay back his grandfather for everything he'd done to raise them.

As much as Martin Quinn wanted his grandsons to go out into the world and find their own dreams, he loved having them home, too. The company ran better with the four of them at full speed.

Dermot picked up his cell phone and hit the memory dial for Rachel. If he were stuck in traffic, then he'd find something pleasant to occupy his time. But, to his surprise, she didn't pick up. Instead, one of the boys answered.

"Hey, is this Trevor?"

"Nope, Taylor."

"Taylor, it's Dermot. How are things going? You working hard?"

"Our mom is living here now," Taylor said. "She's learning how to milk the goats. And she's making soap to sell. And Aunt Rachel hired a guy to help with the milking. Did she tell you that?"

"She did. How's he getting along?"

"He's not as fun as you. He hardly says anything. His name is Leroy and he has a tattoo, but Eddie likes him because he was in the Navy and so was Eddie."

Dermot chuckled. He'd heard all the news from Rachel, but Taylor seemed determined to fill him in. "How are the goats?"

"Benny jumped into the truck yesterday when Aunt Rachel was taking Trevor out for a driving lesson. And Aunt Rachel says that the goats will start having babies in March. I think you should come and see us."

"Is your aunt Rachel there?"

A long silence came over the line and Dermot waited for an answer. "She's not here right now," Taylor said. "But she told us if you called we should tell you that she would talk to you later."

"All right. I'll talk to her later. Say hi to Trevor for me. And be good for your mom, okay?"

He turned the phone off after they said their good-byes and tossed it onto the seat. Just as he did, the traffic began to move. He drove slowly at first, and then, once he passed the scene of a disabled semi-truck, it picked up to normal speeds.

Dermot pulled into his parking spot at the end of the pier and grabbed his briefcase, then stepped out of the car. He hadn't made any plans for the weekend. Nothing seemed to appeal when it came to social activities. His brothers had been as preoccupied as he had since their return and they'd barely had time to speak, much less meet for a beer or a ball game.

He fumbled in his pocket for his key and shoved it in the dead bolt. The lock clicked.

"Dermot?"

The voice was so soft, at first he thought he'd imagined it. He closed his eyes and pushed the door open.

"Dermot?"

There it was again. But this time, it sounded real,

present. He slowly turned to find Rachel standing on the dock. His breath caught in his throat and he stared at her for a long moment. She was like a vision, a beautiful angel with spun gold hair and green eyes.

He dropped his briefcase and crossed the distance between them in a few long steps. Grabbing her in his arms, Dermot picked her up off her feet and gave her a fierce hug. "Holy hell," he said. "What are you doing here?"

He didn't give her time to answer. Instead, he cupped her face in his hands and kissed her. She was everything he remembered her to be, soft, sweet, the perfect fit in his arms. Dermot drew back and looked down into her eyes. "I can't believe it's you. I've been thinking about you all day."

"Is it all right that I came?"

"What? Of course. Are you kidding? I'm so damned happy to see you I can hardly breathe." Dermot kissed her again. "God, you're so beautiful." Suddenly, he realized the significance of her arrival. "I just talked to Taylor. He didn't tell me you were coming."

"I wanted it to be a surprise."

Dermot nodded. "It's a big surprise."

"Now that Jane is living at the farm, I kind of have my life back. She and the boys have decided to stay. I can leave."

Dermot gasped, the news a complete shock. His mind scrambled to take it all in. Could she come to

Seattle and live with him? Did she even want to live with him?

"What does this mean?"

"It means that I'm here. For as long as you want me. I was hanging on to the farm because of the promise I made to my father. But now that my sister is there, it's all in good hands. Since you left, I've been really lonely."

He smiled down at her. "Me, too. I don't like being so far away from you." Dermot took her hands in his. "Rachel, I'm in love with you. There is no other woman for me. And I really can't imagine living my life without you. And now that you're here, I'm not going to let you go."

"I don't want to go," she said. "Well, I do have to go back to Wisconsin. Jane still hasn't gone through a season of kidding, so I have to be there in the late winter to early spring. But I was thinking we could go back together. Kind of like a vacation?"

"You have this all worked out," he said.

"I do."

"I think it's a good plan. I think it's exactly what I've been hoping for."

She threw her arms around his neck and gave him a fierce hug. Dermot laughed, then picked her up and carried her inside the house. He'd dreamed about having her in his arms again, but he never thought it would be this simple.

"I love you, Rachel."

"And I love you, Dermot Quinn."

"Are you going to miss your goats?" he asked.

She stared up at him with sparkling eyes. "They're in the best hands. They have a wonderful family to look after them. And they're going to live happily ever after."

"And what about us?"

"I think we're going to have a wonderful life together. And I want it to begin now."

"What do you want?" He expected her to demand that he take her directly to bed and make love to her. But he was surprised by her request.

"I want to find a quiet place to watch the sunset," she said. "I want to hold your hand and take a deep breath and let this all sink in for a moment."

"I know the perfect place," he said. "You've never been sailing, have you?"

She shook her head. "Is your favorite place on the water?" she asked.

"My favorite place is wherever you are, Rachel. That's the way it will always be."

He took her hand and led her out the front door. And as they walked down the dock, Dermot said a silent thanks to his grandfather for knowing exactly what he needed—a chance to see his life through different eyes. A chance to go out and find his dreams. And a chance to find the love of his life.

He'd never believed it before, but Dermot was certain of it now. He had the luck of the Irish.

* * * * *

COMING NEXT MONTH from Harlequin® Blaze™
AVAILABLE AUGUST 21, 2012

#705 NORTHERN RENEGADE
Alaskan Heat
Jennifer LaBrecque
Former Gunnery Sergeant Liam Reinhardt thinks he's fought his last battle when he rolls into the small town of Good Riddance, Alaska, on the back of his motorcycle. Then he meets Tansy Wellington....

#706 JUST ONE NIGHT
The Wrong Bed
Nancy Warren
Realtor Hailey Fleming is surprised to find a sexy stranger fast asleep in the house she's just listed. Rob Klassen is floored—his house *isn't* for sale—and convincing Hailey of that *and* his good intentions might keep them up all night!

#707 THE MIGHTY QUINNS: KIERAN
The Mighty Quinns
Kate Hoffmann
When Kieran Quinn comes to the rescue of a beautiful blonde, all he expects is a thank-you. But runaway country star Maddie West is on a quest to find herself. And Kieran, with his sexy good looks and killer smile, is the perfect traveling companion.

#708 FULL SURRENDER
Uniformly Hot!
Joanne Rock
Photographer Stephanie Rosen really needs to get her mojo back. And who better for the job than the guy who rocked her world five years ago, navy lieutenant Daniel Murphy?

#709 UNDONE BY MOONLIGHT
Flirting with Justice
Wendy Etherington
As Calla Tucker uncovers the truth about her detective friend Devin Antonio's suspension, more secrets are revealed, including their long, secret attraction for each other....

#710 WATCH ME
Stepping Up
Lisa Renee Jones
A "curse" has hit TV's hottest reality dance show and security chief Sam Kellar is trying to keep control. What he can't control, though, is his desire for Meagan Tippan, the show's creator!

You can find more information on upcoming Harlequin® titles, free excerpts and more at www.Harlequin.com.

HBCNM0812

REQUEST YOUR FREE BOOKS!
2 FREE NOVELS PLUS 2 FREE GIFTS!

red-hot reads!

HARLEQUIN®

SYTYCW

SO YOU THINK YOU CAN WRITE

Harlequin and Mills & Boon are joining forces in a global search for new authors.

In September 2012 we're launching our biggest contest yet—with the prize of being published by the world's leader in romance fiction!

Look for more information on our website,
www.soyouthinkyoucanwrite.com

So you think you can write? Show us!

SYTYCW0912

Enjoy this sneak peek of USA TODAY *bestselling author*
Maureen Child's newest title
UP CLOSE AND PERSONAL

Available September 2012 from Harlequin® Desire!

"Laura, I know you're in there!"

Ronan Connolly pounded on the bright blue front door,
then paused to listen. Not a sound from inside the house,
though he knew too well that Laura was in there. Hell, he
could practically *feel* her standing just on the other side of
the damned door.

He glanced at her car parked alongside the house, then
glared again at the still-closed front door.

"You won't convince me you're not at home. Your car is
parked in the street, Laura."

Her voice came then, muffled but clear. "It's a driveway
in America, Ronan. You're not in Ireland, remember?"

"More's the pity." He scrubbed one hand across his face
and rolled his eyes in frustration. If they were in Ireland
right now, he'd have half the village of Dunley on his side
and he'd bloody well get her to open the door.

"I heard that," she said.

Grinding his teeth together, he counted to ten. Then did
it a second time. "Whatever the hell you want to call it,
Laura, your car is *here* and so are you. Why not open the
door and we can talk this out. Together. In private."

"I've got nothing to say to you."

He laughed shortly. That would be a first indeed, he told
himself. A more opinionated woman he had never met. He
had to admit, he had enjoyed verbally sparring with her. He
admired a quick mind and a sharp tongue. He'd admired her
even more once he'd gotten her into his bed.

He glanced down at the dozen red roses he held clutched in his right hand and called himself a damned fool for thinking this woman would be swayed by pretty flowers and a smooth speech. Hell, she hadn't even *seen* the flowers yet. At this rate, she never would.

Huffing out an impatient breath, he lowered his voice. "You know why I'm here. Let's get it done and have it over then."

There was a moment's pause, as if she were thinking about what he'd said. Then she spoke up again. "You can't have him."

"What?"

"You heard me."

Ronan narrowed his gaze fiercely on the door as if he could see through the panel to the woman beyond. "Aye, I heard you. Though, I don't believe it. I've come for what's mine, Laura, and I'm not leaving until I have it."

Will Ronan get what he's come for?

Find out in Maureen Child's new title
UP CLOSE AND PERSONAL

Available September 2012 from Harlequin® Desire!

Harlequin *Blaze*

red-hot reads

This navy lieutenant is about to get a blast from the past…and start thinking about the future.

Joanne Rock

captivates with another installment of

Men Out of Uniform

Five years ago, photojournalist Stephanie Rosen was kidnapped in a foreign country. Now, with her demons firmly behind her she is ready to move on…and to rev up her sex life! There's only one man she wants, friend and old flame, navy lieutenant Daniel Murphy. Their one night of passion years ago still leaves Stephanie breathless, and with Daniel on leave she's determined to give him a homecoming to remember.

FULL SURRENDER

Available this September wherever books are sold!